# Through the Dragon's Eye

*Christine* and *Christopher* Russell

Published by BBC Educational Publishing,
BBC White City, 201 Wood Lane, London W12 7TS

First published 1991
Reprinted 1991, 1992, 1993, 1994, 1996, 1997
© Christine and Christopher Russell/BBC Enterprises Limited
1990

The moral right of the author has been asserted
Illustrations © Chris Burke 1991
Cover and book design by Jo Digby

ISBN 0 563 34771 6

Set in Baskerville 12/15 by Ace Filmsetting Ltd, Frome, Somerset
Printed and bound in Great Britain by Clays Ltd, St Ives plc

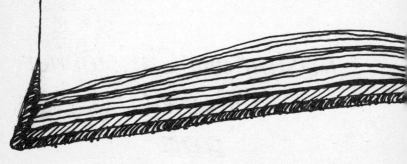

# Contents

# 1 The dragon from Pelamar

It really was a brilliant dragon. Tall and green and scaly, standing beside a waterfall. The rest of the painting was pretty good too. Mountains and streams, flowers and toadstools, a white house in the distance. A whole fairy-tale landscape, in fact—all over the playground wall. A mural, that's what Miss Taylor called it.

Scott, Jenny and Amanda stood back and looked at it. There was only one thing missing: the dragon's eye. And this was Jenny's big moment.

'It's the most important bit,' she told the others as she climbed onto a chair, brush in hand. 'Paintings come alive if you do the eyes properly.'

'Yeah,' said Scott, with a big sarcastic smile, 'he'll be able to watch us and breathe fire . . .'

Jenny just ignored him. Very carefully she dotted in the black centre of the dragon's eye. But as she stepped down beside the other two, the smile slowly faded from Scott's face. The eye winked. And as the children stared, a slight puff of smoke curled from the dragon's nostrils. And it spoke.

'Good morning. It is good to meet you, Amanda . . . Jenny . . . Scott.'

It was a low, rumbling sort of voice. Strong but not unkind. The dragon had turned his head now and was leaning towards them out of the mural. 'Please, don't be afraid . . . Come in . . . There's a path behind the waterfall . . .'

As they stared, real water began to tinkle and splash down the playground wall. Down the waterfall *they* had painted.

It all seemed perfectly natural to the dragon. 'It's quite safe,' he said, 'I will meet you on the other side . . .' And he gazed at them.

Amanda was the first to move. She walked slowly towards the waterfall. That didn't surprise Scott. Amanda was always the one to rush in without thinking. But then Jenny followed her and that *was* a shock. Timid Jenny walking off behind a magic waterfall?

'Scott?' The dragon was still looking at him.

'Come on, Scott.' That was Amanda now, calling from somewhere beyond the waterfall.

'All right, I'm coming.' Scott tried to sound cool and casual, but his knees were shaking as he moved.

Beyond the waterfall was a meadow full of

flowers and toadstools, with mountains in the distance. Jenny and Amanda were gazing around in wonder.

'It's our mural . . .' whispered Jenny, 'come alive.'

The dragon was there as well.

'Welcome to Pelamar. My name is Gorwen . . .' He breathed a puff of smoke, then gravely offered his claw to each of the children in turn. A scaly, green claw, hard and cold and bony, but they shook it anyway—even Scott.

'Look,' cried Amanda, 'it's the flowers I painted.'

And there they were, a row of large red and white blooms. But when Amanda touched one, it instantly collapsed.

'Oh!' Amanda jumped back guiltily and turned to Gorwen. 'It just . . .'

'It just died,' said Gorwen grimly. He didn't sound surprised.

'But why?' asked Jenny.

'Because something dreadful has happened in Pelamar. The Veetacore has exploded.'

Scott frowned. 'The Veetacore? What's that?'

'The Veetacore is everything,' said Gorwen. 'Without its rays we cannot exist. May I show you?'

Amanda and Jenny looked at each other and Amanda nodded. Scott wished they wouldn't keep making up their minds so quickly. He took out his notebook and started to write. Writing helped him think. There was certainly plenty to think about.

'Let us go to the pool,' said Gorwen, and he started to move back towards the waterfall. Amanda and Jenny followed, so Scott found himself on his own again.

'Hey, wait for me!' he yelled after them.

The pool was in a grotto, a small cave behind the waterfall. Amanda and Jenny were staring down into the pool when Scott joined them.

'Well, what *is* this Veetacore?' he asked.

Gorwen blew fire gently on the water. As it rippled, the dark surface glowed golden, and gold was reflected on the children's faces. Looking down into the water, they could see a strange-shaped object, a sort of hexagon, big and golden and dazzlingly bright.

'Wow!' said Scott softly, and the others were thinking the same.

'*That* is the Veetacore,' said Gorwen, 'the life force of Pelamar.'

'It looks all right to me,' said Amanda.

'But you are not looking at it as it is *now*. This is just . . . an image.' The dragon blew more fire on the water. 'Watch again . . .'

This time they could see the Veetacore more clearly. It was standing in a room, glowing, and humming faintly, like a powerful machine. Also in the room was a book. A huge old book on a stand. The book was closed and covered in dust and cobwebs. Around the rest of the room there were cupboards and workbenches, a table and chairs. And in one of the chairs, a rocking chair, was a completely green man.

Green clothes, green hair, green skin. He was knitting with orange wool, which matched the man practising cricket strokes next to him. *He* was orange from head to foot. And over by the Veetacore itself was a purple woman with glasses.

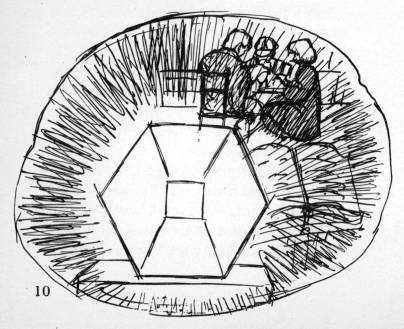

'You are now seeing the Keepers of the Veetacore,' said Gorwen. 'It was their job to look after it. Their names are Doris, Boris and Morris.'

'What's that book?' asked Scott. 'The dusty one?'

'That is the Book of the Veetacore. It tells how to care for the Veetacore and keep it safe . . . Now the pool will show you what happened just a few days ago . . .'

More fire swept gently across the pool. When it cleared, the Keepers were seated at their table in the corner of the room. They turned from their meal as the humming of the Veetacore changed tone and became louder and louder. They looked concerned as the Veetacore began to turn and spin, faster and faster. But as Boris, the orange Keeper, got up from his seat, the Veetacore seemed to explode. The children blinked and closed their eyes, briefly dazzled by the whirling, whizzing storm of gold. And then the pool was dark and still again.

A shocked Amanda looked up at Gorwen. 'Why did it explode?'

'We do not know.' As usual, Gorwen's voice was calm and grave. 'But without the Veetacore there can be no Pelamar. We will all fade and die—just like that flower outside.' He looked at the three children.

'I fear that only *you* can save us.'

There was a moment's silence as they stared back.

'Us?' asked Jenny.

'How?'

Gorwen didn't answer Scott's question straight away. There was more to tell first.

'After the explosion, the Keepers went in search of the scattered pieces.'

'Weren't they hurt?' Amanda butted in.

'No. Nobody was hurt. The Keepers have found all the pieces of the Veetacore *and* they have the Book to tell them what to do . . . But what if they cannot read the Book? No one else in Pelamar can read. The Keepers *should* be able to, but I have grave doubts . . .'

'No one in Pelamar can read? You're joking.' Scott was so surprised he almost laughed.

Gorwen shook his head slowly. 'No. Through the ages we have just . . . forgotten how.'

A phone rang somewhere, and to the children's amazement the dragon unhooked a green, scaly videophone from under his wing and spoke into it. 'Rodey? How did you get on?'

'Useless!' replied a squeaky, angry voice. 'Doris wouldn't even let me in the Veetacore

House. Gorwen, we must *do* something.'

Gorwen turned the videophone screen towards the children. They found themselves face to face with a giant white mouse. It stared at them, and they stared back.

'That is why I have invited Jenny, Scott and Amanda from the other world,' said the dragon. 'Rodey, go back to the Veetacore House. I shall meet you there as soon as I can.'

Gorwen replaced his videophone and blew on the pool again. 'Let us see what the Keepers are doing *now* . . .'

Actually, they didn't seem to be doing very much. Various pieces of the Veetacore, all different shapes and sizes but all still glowing dimly, were scattered around the room. Boris was using one of them as a wicket for bowling practice. Morris, meanwhile, was feeding his pets—a giant pink snail and a turquoise tortoise. Only Doris seemed at all concerned about the disaster. The Book of the Veetacore was open on its stand and she was in front of it, glasses on the end of her nose, blowing dust off a page.

'I am *not* doing this on my own!' Doris stamped her foot and glared at the other two Keepers. They looked at each other and trailed over to where she was standing.

'Thank you.' She nodded curtly, closed
the Book and thrust it into Boris's arms.
'Now, Boris, you read the Book and *I'll* start
putting the bits together.'

Boris didn't seem at all keen on this idea.

'No, no,' he said hastily, pushing it back.
'You read the Book and I'll put . . .'

'No, no, no . . .' Doris was thrusting the
Book at Morris now. 'Morris, *you* read it.'

'I can't—the dust makes my eyes water.'
And he passed it on to Boris. It was like a
game of pass the parcel.

'*I* can't because I haven't got my glasses,'
declared Boris, pushing the book back into
Doris's hands.

'Boris,' she said, 'you don't *wear* glasses.'

But she didn't try to get rid of the Book
again. She put it back on its stand and
opened it. The only trouble was, it was
upside down. None of the Keepers seemed
to notice. After an awkward look at each
other, they peered down at it together,
frowning hard . . .

'Know what I think?' said Scott to
Gorwen. 'I think you're in big trouble.'

The pool had gone dark and still again.
Amanda turned to the anxious dragon. 'I
don't think any of them can read. Not even
Doris.'

Gorwen looked at the children.

'So, will you help us? Will *you* read the Book?'

Jenny felt worried. She wasn't a very confident reader. But she wasn't going to be the one to say no, especially with Gorwen looking so anxious.

The children glanced at each other and this time Scott took the lead, with one of his cool, casual shrugs.

'Sure. Why not.'

'Thank you!' rumbled the dragon, with obvious relief. 'Now, are you ready to fly?'

Suddenly Scott didn't feel so cool and casual any more.

The flying wasn't so bad, really. Gorwen's back was broad. There was plenty of room for three. And a dragon's scales are handy things to hold onto. Amanda loved it, and even Scott had opened his eyes before they circled down to land outside the Veetacore House.

The House was in a meadow much the same as the one by the waterfall, except that there were a few fallen trees lying around and one or two which looked dead although they were still standing. The House itself, with its white walls and its green doors and shutters, was exactly the same as the one in the playground mural. None of the children was a bit surprised at this. They were getting used to Pelamar.

'Come, my friends, let us go inside,' said Gorwen, glancing at the fallen trees and some other rubble nearby. 'This may have become a High Fade Zone.'

'What's that?' asked Amanda.

'A place where buildings collapse or plants and creatures just fade away. It can happen very suddenly, without warning.'

'Look!' cried Amanda.

For a moment the children saw all three Keepers staring out of the windows of the Veetacore House. Then they suddenly disappeared and the shutters slammed shut.

Gorwen unhooked his videophone with a weary sigh. 'Oh dear, this is going to be difficult.'

Inside the Veetacore House Doris glared at Gorwen's face on the House video screen. Then she saw other faces appear beside Gorwen's. Strange, sickly faces that she didn't recognise. One of them spoke.

'The Book's still upside down, Gorwen.'

Doris hastily turned the Book round, but she was still determined not to let anyone in.

Then Jenny screamed, 'Gorwen, the tree!'

As she spoke, a large tree standing close to

the Veetacore House began to sway and fall. Gorwen raised his wing to shield the children, and the tree crashed down against the doors of the Veetacore House, bursting them open. The dragon paused for only a moment, recovering from the near miss.

'Inside!' he cried, and the children followed him into the House.

Doris was standing by the Book. She was still defiant.

'How dare you come in here! *We* are the Keepers of the Veetacore and *we* have everything under control.'

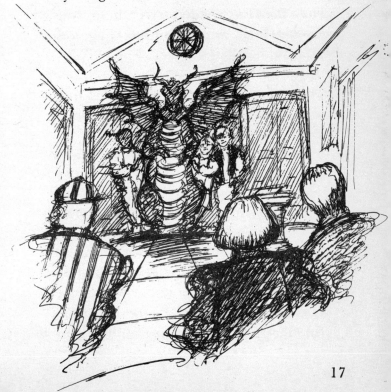

'No, Doris, you have nothing under control!' Gorwen was breathing smoke. 'Let me speak. We *must* get the Veetacore together again quickly.' He turned to the children, grouped behind him. 'My friends from the other world *can* read. For the sake of Pelamar, let them see the Book!'

Boris obviously felt he ought to support Doris.

'We can do it without the stupid old Book,' he said.

'It is impossible without the Book!' rumbled the exasperated dragon.

Then the House video screen lit up with fuzzy grey lines, and a loud crackling noise came from it. Then a voice:

'Keepers! The Great West . . .'

The voice was drowned in crackles and whines, then words began to appear on the screen.

'Interference again,' said Doris, irritably. 'Turn it off, Morris.'

'No don't,' cried Scott. 'It's a message.' And he hurried over to the screen, followed closely by Morris. 'Can you turn the sound down, please?'

'A message without sound and pictures?' scoffed Boris.

Doris obviously felt the same. 'It's just a lot of black and white squiggles.' But she

18

didn't stop Morris from turning down the sound. A word message was left on the screen:

Keepers !
Great West Lake
now High Fade Zone.
Nothing left alive.
Keep away!  Please!

But when Amanda read the message to them, the Keepers were suspicious.

'How do we know she's telling the truth?' asked Morris.

'Yes, how?' said Doris. 'She's making it up.'

Gorwen groaned but before he could speak, Rodey, the giant white mouse, had scrambled past the fallen tree and into the House.

'Gorwen, Gorwen, thank goodness! I'm sorry I'm late. I flew over the Great West Lake. It's awful—everything there is dead!'

The Keepers looked startled. They glanced at each other.

'We know,' said Gorwen quietly. He looked at Doris. 'Is this the proof you need?'

Doris didn't reply immediately. She wasn't just obstinate, she was proud.

Suddenly, she turned to the Book stand, her arms folded. 'Well, get on with it!'

The children moved quickly to join her, then hesitated. Doris was just standing there. Jenny looked up at her shyly and tried to touch the Book, but Doris obviously didn't want her to.

'Uh, we have to start at the beginning . . .' said Jenny politely.

Without a word, Doris flicked rapidly back through the pages. Inside the front cover was printed in big letters:

# The Veetacore of Pelamar

Doris looked sharply at Jenny, who was still afraid to touch the Book.

'Uh, page one?' said Jenny.

Doris turned one page and looked at her again.

'Yes . . .' Jenny tried a smile. 'Thank you.'

But Doris didn't return the smile. She stepped back and regarded the children stonily as they crowded round and peered at the text on page one.

'I knew it,' wailed Jenny. 'I can't read a word.' And deep inside she felt the churning in her stomach which she always felt when a page full of long words stared up at her.

'Don't panic,' whispered Amanda firmly. 'Take it slowly, right?'

It wasn't just that the words were long. The print was so old-fashioned. Even the short words seemed hard to read. Scott had a go. Concentrating hard, he read out loud:

'The Veetacore is constructed in such a way that every component part, or Veeton, is relative to, and dependent on, another. The Veetons, which have no power in isolation, number twenty-five in total.'

'D'you understand it, Scott?' asked Amanda.

Scott shrugged. 'Only that there are twenty-five bits and they're called Veetons.'

'Well, that's a start,' said Amanda, determined to be positive, and she moved away to count the glowing pieces of Veetacore scattered about the room.

Scott and Jenny were left to puzzle over the meaning of that first paragraph in the Book.

'Relative to and dependent on another,' muttered Scott.

'Relative—something to do with a family?' Jenny wasn't very confident, even when she thought she was right. 'Like a family: goes together? Depends on each other?'

Scott was looking at her. 'Yeah,' he said.

'That could be it—you've got to get the right bits next to each other.'

'Scott?' Amanda had finished counting and was calling across to him. She looked anxious. 'Did you say twenty-*five* Veetons?'

'Yes, definitely,' said Scott, checking again in the Book. 'Twenty-five in total.'

Amanda pulled a grim face. 'Well, there are only twenty-*two* here.'

## Flight to Widge

For a mouse, Rodey could get very cross.

'You said you had them all!' he squeaked at the Keepers. 'You said you'd searched the whole of Pelamar!'

'We did,' said Boris stoutly. 'Every centimetre.'

'Every millimetre,' nodded Morris.

'Every, every . . .' Boris couldn't remember what came after millimetres, if anything. 'Every*where*.'

'They cannot have vanished,' rumbled Gorwen. 'If they are not in Pelamar, then they must have fallen beyond the mountains . . . in Widge.'

The Pelamots all stared at Gorwen in horror.

'In Widge?' gasped Rodey. 'Oh no . . . not in Widge. Please, not Widge.'

'Rodey.' Gorwen spoke sharply, but the mouse was not to be stopped.

'But it's an awful place. The air's so thin you can't fly. The weather changes every minute. It's nothing but tricks and traps and Widgets!'

The children were bewildered.

'What? . . . Widgets?'

'Well,' said Boris, 'the Widgets are . . .' But he couldn't find the right word.

'The Widgets,' said Morris gloomily.

'And if they've got their furry fingers on the Veetons,' squeaked Rodey, 'we shall never get them back!'

'We *have* to get them back,' said Gorwen simply. 'A search party must set out at once. I will go. Who will come with me?'

None of the Keepers volunteered. It was Amanda who broke the awkward silence.

'I'll go with you.' Then she turned. 'Scott?'

Why did she *have* to keep putting him on the spot like this? She didn't seem to understand that some people prefer to think things over for a bit.

'It'd be like a quest,' Amanda continued. 'Like in the storybooks you're always reading—a search for something really important.'

'I'd like to go.' That was Jenny now. What was the matter with *her*. Pelamar seemed to have gone to her head.

Scott shrugged. 'All right.' Then he had a sudden thought and added hopefully, 'But someone'll have to stay here—to read the Book.'

'You're right,' nodded Amanda. 'Got three pencils? We'll draw lots.'

Unfortunately he did have three pencils. And, even more unfortunately, when Morris held them out in his fist, Scott drew the longest—even though he had first pick. Jenny drew the shortest, which meant she stayed in the Veetacore House. She was obviously disappointed—and worried.

'I'm not the best reader, that's the trouble.'

'You'll be fine,' smiled Amanda. 'Just have a go.'

And there wasn't a lot Scott could do about it.

Gorwen was glowering at the Keepers now, trying to shame them into action.

'One of the Keepers *must* come with us. Two will stay with Jenny . . .'

He even breathed a little smoke to help them make up their minds. But Amanda had an easier solution.

'Ip, dip, sky blue, who goes, not you. Ip, dip, sky blue, who goes, not you. You win, Boris. You're coming to Widge.'

'What? But . . .'

So the search party was decided: Gorwen, Amanda, Scott, Boris—and Rodey.

'You're coming too?' Amanda was surprised.

Rodey held his head high. 'Of course. *I* am the only Pelamot who can speak

Widgeon. No quest to Widge could succeed without me.'

Gorwen was turning briskly to the door. 'Let us be on our way. There is no time to lose.'

Boris grumbled and fumbled in a store cupboard, loading supplies into his rucksack, then he fussed around looking for his cricket bat.

'Thank you,' he nodded curtly, as Jenny handed the bat to him.

Scott had also found something—a map of Widge. But Boris wasn't interested. He simply took Amanda by the hand and marched outside. 'Right, hold tight and when I say run, you run, okay?' He pointed the bat at the evening sky. 'Run!'

And Amanda felt herself yanked forward before she had time to ask questions or feel scared. The next thing she knew, she and Boris were soaring through the air and Jenny's voice was floating up from far below.

'Bye . . .'

'Bye, Jenny . . . Good luck . . .'

Gorwen was also airborne, with Scott on his back, and now Rodey came up alongside, flying with a strange sort of doggy-paddle action. Boris was beginning to enjoy himself.

'Widge!' he shouted. 'Here we come!'

Left alone at the window of the Veetacore
House, Jenny felt suddenly sad and worried.
And frightened—even though Widge
sounded more dangerous than Pelamar. She
shivered slightly.

'What's the matter—cold?' Doris was
standing behind her. She didn't sound very
friendly.

Jenny shrugged. 'Just for a second, yes—I
felt sort of shivery.'

Doris crossed to the Book stand.

'Well, come on then,' she said briskly,
'tell me what to do.'

But when Jenny joined her at the open
Book, there was more to worry about than

just the words. A caterpillar was eating holes in the page.

'Frug! *There* you are, you naughty caterpillar,' said Morris, picking up the tiny pet and stroking it gently. 'He's only a baby. Say hello to Jenny, Frug.'

'A baby? How big will he grow then?'

'Oh, normal Pelamot size,' said Morris rather vaguely, and he wandered off again.

'You shouldn't let him eat the Book, you know,' said Jenny. But it was difficult to get cross with Morris.

'I'm still waiting.' That was Doris. It wouldn't be difficult to get cross with her. Jenny was determined to stand up for herself. She gave Doris a look, then concentrated hard on studying the Book. The words on the page seemed to merge together. She ran her finger slowly over them, muttering slightly, trying to make some sense of it all.

'Sometimes it is necessary to expose the core for maintenance purposes. The four tri . . .'

Part of the next word was missing. Jenny looked beyond it and was excited to find that she could understand the rest of the sentence.

'. . . Veetons make up the base . . .' The four *what* Veetons make up the base, though? The most important word on the whole page and that caterpillar had eaten it. Tri . . . 'tri' what? Jenny could feel the panic rising inside her. She didn't want to panic. Especially with Doris watching her. And then a strange thing happened. Jenny couldn't explain it to the others properly when she told them about it later. It wasn't that the Book actually *spoke* to her. And yet, she could hear words in her head, and for some reason she was sure the Book was putting them there. The Book was trying to help.

'Let's think . . .' Jenny was talking out loud. 'The Veetons are made in lots of sizes and *shapes*—shapes. Is it about shapes? Tri . . . tri . . . tripe? No. Tricyle. No, that's not a shape . . . Triangle! *That's* a shape all right! Tri-ang-ular! What a helpful Book. The four *triangular* Veetons make up the base! See, Doris? Like this!'

And, taking her notebook from her pocket, she went to the table and started to draw four triangles fitting together to form a rectangle. But Doris still refused to be impressed.

'Well, why draw pictures when you can read?' she asked irritably.

'Sometimes you need words *and* pictures,' smiled Jenny. She was suddenly happy and confident. She wanted Doris to like and trust her.

'Tell you what, Doris, why don't you and I rewrite the hard bits of the Book as we work them out?'

Doris clutched the Book to her chest in shock.

'Rewrite the Book! No!'


Boris's version of flying was a bit different from Gorwen's. Gorwen flew in a straight line. So did Rodey. Boris found straight lines boring, so he weaved left and right, up and down, all the time.

'Now this is *really* clever,' he yelled. 'Flying's better than silly old reading any day!' And with that, he started looping the loop. Amanda squealed, half frightened, half delighted, as the ground far below seemed to turn upside-down.

'And now a triple loop the loop!'

And away they went again, spinning over and over. And over and over . . . Amanda became suddenly alarmed, clinging on for dear life as she sensed Boris losing control of his speed and direction. She screamed and shut her eyes.

'Boris!'

'Ooohhh . . .!'

The crash wasn't as bad as Amanda expected. No bones broken. When she sat up, she found herself in a field. Not green but soft and dusty, with even more fallen trees than around the Vectacore House. Boris lay in a groaning heap beside her.

'Well, that wasn't so clever, was it?' said Amanda. 'And you've broken your bat.'

Actually, it wasn't broken, just a bit split at the end, but Boris sat up at once and was examining it nervously as Rodey, Gorwen and Scott landed close by.

'What have you done now?' squeaked Rodey. 'If you've damaged your bat, you know you can't fly without it!'

'Don't be cross,' pleaded Amanda. 'Anyway, I think it's time we stopped for something to eat.'

So they did. But Boris wasn't allowed anything. He took a roll of sticky tape from the rucksack and sat down to mend his bat, and sulk.

'Figs . . . dates . . . peanuts . . .' Amanda was taking labelled tubs from the rucksack and offering them to the others. She put an open tub of strawberries a little too close to Boris and, with a crafty glance, he shot out a hand and took one. But which was the sugar and which was the salt? Two labelled tubs with white stuff in them stood beside the strawberries. Boris made a guess, dunked his strawberry and popped it in his mouth quickly. Then promptly spat it out again.

'Ugh!'

The others turned as he coughed and spluttered in disgust. Amanda was concerned.

'What's the matter, Boris?'

'These strawberries—they're *awful*.'

Amanda guessed what had happened. 'They'd be nicer with sugar on them,' she smiled sweetly, 'instead of salt.' She picked up the labelled sugar and salt tubs and held them next to each other. 'Perhaps reading's not so silly after all.'

And everyone laughed—except Boris, whose head started ringing. Well, not exactly his head, but the cricket cap *on* his head. There was a videophone in its peak.

'Look, Scott,' cried Amanda. 'That's neat.'

'Is it?' said Boris, gazing briefly at the interference on the screen before tossing the cap aside. 'Would be if it worked.'

'If this is a High Fade Zone, it's bound not to work,' said Rodey. And he went back to nibbling peanuts.

Amanda picked up the cap and was delighted to see Jenny's face gradually appearing on the screen.

'Hi, Jenny. How are you getting on?'

With the four triangular Veetons fitted together on their plinth, Jenny was getting on fine.

'But Doris isn't being too helpful,' she said quietly. 'And it's getting so cold. Are you cold?'

Amanda was surprised. 'No. It's a nice warm evening here.'

'It's strange,' puzzled Jenny. 'As soon as Gorwen left, it got cold . . . more sort of shivery than cold, really . . . I don't like it . . .'

But as Amanda turned to ask Gorwen about this, she noticed Rodey, who had wandered a little way off. Or rather, she noticed the ground behind Rodey. She could see right through him.

'Rodey!' she screamed. 'Rodey's fading!'

'Get away from here! Hurry!' roared Gorwen, scattering the picnic with his tail as he crouched down for Scott and Amanda to scramble onto his back. But as Boris grabbed the rucksack, there was a shrill squeak. And there before him on the ground was a solid but very tiny white mouse.

'Rodey, is that you?'

'Of course it's me! Get me out of here before I get any smaller!'

Boris plucked up the tiny creature by the tail, raised his bat and ran.

In the Veetacore House a bewildered Jenny was gazing at the blank video screen.

'Must have been a High Fade Zone,' said a worried-looking Morris.

Indeed it must. Gorwen, with Scott and Amanda clinging to his back, flew fast and high, far away from danger, before turning and calling to the orange Keeper close behind him.

'Is Rodey safe, Boris?'

'Yes,' Boris listened to the muffled squeaks coming from his pocket. 'He says he can't grow again, though. The power's gone.'

'He'll still be able to talk to the Widgets, won't he?' asked Scott.

'I hope so . . .' Gorwen didn't sound too sure.

'Are the Widgets as bad as Boris says they are?' This was Amanda. She was looking forward to meeting the strange-sounding creatures.

'No,' said Gorwen. 'They're just naughty, I suppose. I'm sure they won't help us.'

Gorwen didn't know it, but as he spoke he was being watched by a bunch of the very creatures he was talking about. Widgets. Bright-eyed, pointy-eared, furry-faced, bouncy-footed, tumble-tummied, squeaking, chippering, jostling, tittering bundles of practical joke. Widgets. The cooking fire of their border camp burning brightly behind them. And in their hands a telescope, through which each in turn—or not in turn if they could get away with it— peered up into the now darkening sky above the mountains.

The stars were out as Gorwen slowed down and then merely hovered, waiting for Boris to draw alongside.

'Which way?' panted Boris, looking around.

'I don't know . . .' replied Gorwen. He too was short of breath. 'We must be very close. The air's getting too thin to fly through.'

'We could do with some road signs,' grunted Scott.

'Sky signs, you mean.' It was just a sort of joke—Amanda didn't expect the sky to do anything about it. But suddenly the stars above them lit up like a brilliant firework display:

## *Beware thin air*

'Look!' cried Amanda, pointing in wonder. 'Sky-writing!'

Then shooting stars seemed to whoosh across the sky in all directions, trailing their messages behind them:

## *Pelamar*
## *Too low*
## *No go*
## *Widge way*

'Widge Way!' shouted Scott, pointing in the direction of the last message.

In the border camp below, the Widgets bounced, rolled and tumbled out of sight, huddling together in the trees, watching with their big, mischievous eyes as the search party landed, came forward into the clearing and stopped.

'Is that them?' whispered Amanda. 'The Widgets?'

'Yep,' said Boris, without enthusiasm. 'That's them all right.'

Gorwen stepped towards the Widgets.

'Greetings from Pelamar,' he rumbled.

The Widgets cowered away.

'They're scared of us!' exclaimed Amanda.

'Little pests,' muttered Boris.

'But they're sweet,' said Amanda.

'Yes,' said Gorwen quietly, 'but do not trust them.' He turned to Boris. 'Where is Rodey?'

Boris produced the tiny white mouse from his pocket and held him out on the palm of his hand.

'Rodey,' said Gorwen, 'tell the Widgets we're their friends and that we need their help.'

Looking towards the Widgets, Rodey began to speak in Widgeon, which sounded to Scott and Amanda rather like every different kind of squeak they'd ever heard, all squashed together and played on a tape at double speed. The Widgets seemed to understand what he was saying, though. They chippered and squeaked loudly amongst themselves for a few seconds, stared suspiciously across the clearing, then advanced together, stopping just in front of Boris and peering at the white mouse on his hand.

Rodey squeaked some more Widgeon at them. The Widgets listened in silence, then moved away a little and went into a squeaking huddle.

'What are they saying?' asked Gorwen anxiously.

'I can't hear from here,' said Rodey, 'but I told them about the Veetacore, that there are three Veetons missing and that we think they are somewhere in Widge.'

The Widgets advanced again and began to make the visitors welcome. Scott and Amanda were led to the fire, while Boris, still carrying Rodey, was invited to sit on a blanket-covered boulder.

'They say we can stay here for the night,' translated Rodey. 'And in the morning they will help us begin the quest.'

'There,' said Amanda. 'They *are* friendly after all.'

'Huh,' scoffed Boris. And he eyed the Widgets warily.

Scott was already spreading out his map of Widge. 'We could start to work out a plan,' he said. 'Now, where are we?'

Amanda looked over his shoulder and pointed. 'Border Camp, I suppose.'

A couple of Widgets were also peeping at the map, but they said nothing.

Scott nodded. 'There are three paths from here. Which one do we take?'

'I don't know,' shrugged Amanda. 'Go for the middle one?' She pointed at the map. 'North?'

One of the Widgets peering at the map held in a titter. He still said nothing, but above his head a thinks bubble popped up—it was just a Widget trick; the sort they played on you if they thought you couldn't read.

'NORTH?' said the bubble.

And answering thoughts popped out of the heads of the Widgets sitting beside Boris:

Rodey saw them and squeaked, 'Boris, look!'

Boris did look. And so did Amanda. Too late. The bubbles burst and the Widgets smiled. A picture of innocence.

# 3
## The first Veeton

Amanda was writing in her notebook while the Border Camp bustled around her. It was early morning. The fire was out and the Widgets were shaking and folding rugs. Scott, with Rodey on his hand, was pointing out on the map which path they were going to follow. Two Widgets who had offered to act as guides were nodding in agreement. Gorwen, patient as always, was watching and waiting for everyone else to be ready. Boris was practising cricket strokes.

Amanda finished her notes. She wasn't a great one for writing but for once she agreed with Scott. If they wrote things down, they'd be able to prove afterwards that this adventure had really happened. If there *was* an afterwards. For the first time she wondered whether they'd ever get home again. Back to the playground and Miss Taylor. She quickly put the worry out of her mind and stood up.

'Rodey,' she called, 'd'you want to go in Boris's pocket again?'

Rodey didn't.

'Boris's pocket smells of old socks,' he complained.

So Amanda put him in *her* pocket, which only smelt of peppermints, and the search party set out. Heading north. Behind the backs of the departing visitors, Widget thinks bubbles popped up all over the place:

*Ha, ha...*

*Good trick!*

Scott felt good. The track through the forest was clear and easy, the Widgets were friendly, and Widge itself didn't seem at all dangerous. With the map in his hand, he could even pretend he was in charge.

'This is what I *call* a quest,' he declared to everyone in general. 'Bet I find the first Veeton.'

'Course you will,' smiled Amanda. But Scott thought she sounded a bit sarcastic.

The two Widget guides were walking backwards, waving to their friends at the Border Camp. Thinks bubbles were floating above their heads:

*Fooled them!*

Boris saw and blinked at the message. He couldn't read and the Widgets knew it. They turned and stared back at him while the bubbles slowly faded and popped.

'Funny lot, these Widgets,' muttered Boris. And he turned on his way.

He didn't realise quite *how* funny. The Widgets at the Border Camp were giving themselves very high marks for funniness. They were clutching each other and rolling helplessly on the ground. Then, just to prove to themselves how right they were about being funny, they whipped a rug from the top of a rock. And there lay a dimly-glowing golden slab, about the size of a very large book. A Veeton. They all collapsed in a chippering, giggling heap again. What made it especially funny was that Boris had been sitting on that rock earlier on.

A small wheelbarrow was trundled over to the rock by one of the few Widgets still able to stand up for laughing, the Veeton was heaved into it and off they all went—in a completely different direction from the search party.

'Do *you* feel cold, Morris?' Jenny had decided to leave Doris alone for a while. Morris wasn't so prickly. He was only interested in his pets Frug, Frenny and Frista, and he was standing at the table now, chopping vegetables for them. Though Frug the caterpillar seemed to be growing at such a rate, Jenny thought he'd soon be able to manage an *un*chopped cabbage quite comfortably.

'Yes,' said Morris, thoughtfully. 'Ever since Gorwen left—cold and damp.'

Doris was over by the base of the Veetacore, the Book in her hand, trying to judge where the next Veetons should fit.

'If we shift this bit,' she said, prodding one of the triangular Veetons, 'that one over there should fit.'

Jenny was close to despair. 'Doris!' she cried, going over to her. 'They have to *stay there*. The Book *says* so. You're just *guessing*. Pelamar will fade away before you even get half of it done.' Jenny didn't want that to happen. Quite apart from anything else, she felt responsible. Everything that *could* be done there in the Veetacore House while the others were in Widge, *had* to be done. It was up to her.

'Doris?' No answer. '*Please*, Doris . . .'

Doris glowered, then suddenly thrust the Book at her.

'Take it.'

Jenny took it. With a relieved, polite smile. But as she quickly  placed the Book on its stand, she turned and said, 'Doris, I need you too. Please help me.'

She could tell Doris didn't really want to be left out, and Jenny didn't want to leave her out either. And although Doris didn't exactly smile, she wasn't quite as sharp as before.

'Well then, you'd better read the next bit.'

Jenny tried. But it wasn't easy.

'The short ky-linder in the centre serves as a support for the large, flat, circular Veeton.'

Doris looked at Jenny, baffled.

'Ky-linder? What's a ky-linder?'

'I'm not sure,' frowned Jenny, getting worried. She looked around at the scattered Veetons and pointed. 'That one's short!'

'Ky-linder?' scoffed Doris, picking it up. 'That's a cylinder.'

'Oh, yeah. Of course it is.'

'Well, go on. Read the next bit.'

Jenny looked down at the Book again.

'. . . serves as a support for the large, flat, circular Veeton.'

'Like this?'

Jenny and Doris turned in surprise. Morris was looking helpfully across at them. In one hand he had a thick cylinder of marrow and on top of it he was placing a slice of pineapple.

'Yeah, that's it,' laughed Jenny. 'This is team work.'

'So let's find one that looks like this,' beamed Morris, holding up the slice of pineapple.

Doris found the circular Veeton, but as she did, Morris looked suddenly alarmed.

'Where's Frug?'

'Doris, check the Book!' cried Jenny.

It was a false alarm. Frug was only on the workbench. But Doris thought she'd found something wrong with the Book anyway.

'Is that page all right?' she frowned.

Jenny examined it.

'It's just a bit of dirt,' she said with relief, and blew the dirt from the page. But something held her eyes.

'Hang on,' she muttered, 'this page seems to be about finding lost Veetons.' She read aloud as best she could:

'In the unlikely event of an explosion "something-ing" a search for missing Veetons, the Veetarods will prove "something-able" and should be trusted at all times.' She looked at Doris. 'What are Veetarods?'

'Veetarods?' Doris searched her memory. 'Veetarods . . . What's a Veetarod, Morris?'

'It's one of those golden things,' said the thoughtful green Keeper.

'Yes,' said Doris, half remembering. 'It tells you when you're close to a Veeton.'

Morris was rummaging in his knitting bag. 'We've each got one,' he muttered. 'Yes, here's mine.'

He held up a folded square of golden metal. Unfolded, it formed a zigzag rod about half a metre long, with two handles at one end. And when he held it towards the nearest Veeton, the rod trembled violently and made an urgent humming noise, rather like a car alarm with the volume turned down.

'Clever, isn't it?' beamed Morris.

'But it's no use here!' cried Jenny. 'Did Boris take one with him?'

She crossed to the videophone and pressed a code button rather impatiently. The screen lit up at once but showed only fuzzy grey interference. 'Oh, come on . . .'

'Try again,' said Morris. 'The whole system seems to be breaking down.'

Then the screen suddenly cleared and Jenny could see and hear Gorwen.

'Gorwen, I've found something in the Book you should know about. Ask Boris if he's got . . .'

And that was all Gorwen heard. Jenny's face broke up on his screen and he was left on the forest path holding a videophone which just crackled and buzzed at him.

'What's up?' asked Scott, as he and Amanda peered over Gorwen's shoulder.

'The interference is getting worse,' said Gorwen. 'The picture's breaking up again.'

Then the screen cleared and words appeared on it:

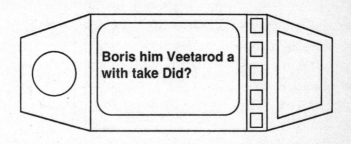

**Boris him Veetarod a with take Did?**

'What's that all about?' frowned Scott.

'Perhaps Jenny was trying to tell us something?' suggested Amanda.

'No, it's got a question mark. It must be a question.' Scott already had his notebook and pencil out. There was nothing he liked better than a puzzle.

'Well, if it's a question,' said Amanda, 'I think "Did" should come first.'

Scott wrote it down. 'Did . . .'

'Did Boris . . . ?' tried Amanda.

'Did Boris what? Take?' Amanda frowned. 'Take . . . Take a Veetarod?'

Scott saw a way to the end and wrote it down quickly:

'Did Boris take a Veetarod with him?' Then he looked blank. 'What's a Veetarod?'

A new jumbled sentence was appearing on Gorwen's screen:

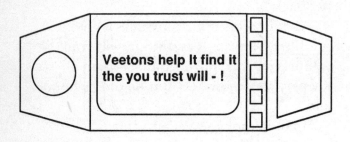

Veetons help It find it
the you trust will - !

Scott and Amanda stared helplessly at the screen, then Amanda pushed a button in annoyance and the message sorted itself out:

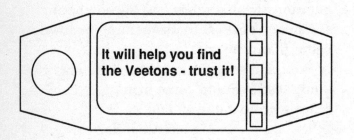

It will help you find
the Veetons - trust it!

Boris had taken no interest in the message puzzle—he was practising cricket strokes again. But he looked up as Gorwen called.

'Boris! Do you know anything about a Veetarod?'

'Of course I do,' he replied carelessly. 'It's a sort of Veeton detector—it trembles when you're near a Veeton. I've got one in my rucksack.'

'What good is it in your rucksack?' rumbled Gorwen. 'Just find it, will you!'

'Boris do this, Boris do that—I am a Keeper, you know . . .' But he did as he was told.

Amanda took the Veetarod. It immediately began to tremble and turn in her hands, pointing away from the main path towards a narrower, more overgrown track on the left. But the Widget guides had already passed this turning and were waiting a little further on.

Scott wanted to follow the Widgets, but Amanda felt they should trust the Veetarod, just as the message from Jenny had said. Gorwen agreed. He nodded towards the overgrown path. 'Boris, your turn to lead.'

Boris peered doubtfully through the leaves. He wasn't any keener than Scott about going into the unknown. But Gorwen just stood looking at him, so in the end he braced himself, turned left and the others followed. But although the Veetarod continued to tremble, eveyone began to doubt whether they were going the right way. The main path had been light and cheerful. Warm sunshine had filtered through bright green leaves. Here on the new path everything was dark and dank. Even the clearing Boris came out into wasn't any better. Dead leaves. Dead wood. Damp ground.

'What a gloomy place,' he muttered.

A large notice board loomed beside him. Boris glanced at it, saw another path on the other side of the clearing and made a big mistake. Because 'DANGER! QUAGMIRE!' doesn't mean a lot to you when you can't read.

'Hey,' he called back to the others, 'the path is this way.'

And he marched straight into a swamp. Not just a wet, claggy swamp, but a greedy swamp. A bottomless, bubbling, suck-you-down swamp.

'Help! Get me out! I'm sinking!'

'Stop!' roared Gorwen, as Scott and Amanda rushed to the rescue. 'Stay away from the edge. The bat. Use his cricket bat!'

Scott held the bat towards Boris's stretching fingers, but Boris couldn't reach it. He was up to his neck now and still sinking.

'Stop panicking, Boris!' Gorwen was roaring again. It was all very well for him.

'It's *your* bat. Use it!'

Boris stared at Gorwen across the ooze, then suddenly realised what he meant.

'Right . . .' He closed his eyes, trying to ignore the glugging of the quagmire as it began to seep into his ears. He clicked his fingers above his head.

'Length, bat, length.'

Nothing happened. He clicked again, desperately.

'Length, bat, length!'

And to Scott's astonishment the cricket bat glowed briefly in his hand and practically doubled in size. Boris grabbed the end, and Scott and Amanda began to haul him out.

To begin with Boris felt as if he were being torn in half. The quagmire didn't seem at all keen to let him go. And when at last he was standing shakily on firm ground again, mucky, soaked but safe, the quagmire continued to seethe and bubble in a cheated sort of way. It was the kind of thing to put you right off a quest.

Scott was puzzled. 'Gorwen,' he asked, 'can the Widgets read?'

'I don't think so. Why?' asked the dragon in surprise.

'Well,' said Scott, pointing at the notice board, 'this is a very important notice, but it's not much use if you can't read.' Behind him the Widgets were sending up a thinks bubble:

'Let's ask Rodey if he knows,' said Amanda, thrusting her hand into her pocket and pulling him out—a little too roughly for the mouse's liking.

'Ow! Knows what?'

'Sorry, Rodey, but we want to know if the Widgets can read. You see, if they *can* read, we could write down any questions we want to ask them. Then we wouldn't need you at all.' It was meant to be a joke, but like a lot of Amanda's jokes, it got taken the wrong way.

'Oh, thanks very much.'

'Sorry, Rodey, I didn't mean it like that . . .'

But Rodey was in a huff now, and when Scott and Amanda shifted a fallen tree trunk into position so that it formed a bridge across the quagmire, he scurried across on his own.

'D'you like the new outfit?'

The others turned. Boris had disappeared briefly to clean himself up. Now he was back. The clean trainers were all right. So were the trousers. But the *jumper* . . . It appeared to have been made from an orange sheep with a freaky hairstyle. Scott considered it briefly.

'Might as well fall back in again,' he grunted.

It wasn't easy getting Gorwen across the log bridge. Dragons aren't built for tightrope walking. But at last they were all safely over and heading away from the gloomy clearing with its greedy, guzzling quagmire.

'That's it, forget about me,' squeaked Rodey, as they marched straight past him. '*I'll* make my own way.'

Nobody noticed the Widget guides either as they scampered away through the trees with 'TIME TO GO!' bubbles fading and popping behind them.

The Widgets were in a hurry. It was time to play hide the Veeton again. In a grassy clearing not too far off was a huge tree, and close to the tree was a mound of snoozing Widgets. And parked in the middle of the snoozing Widgets was the wheelbarrow. Suddenly all was chippering, squeaking confusion as the Widget guides arrived and woke the snoozers, and the wheelbarrow, complete with Veeton, was trundled rapidly towards the tree—and into it. At least, halfway into it, because the barrow and several Widgets got stuck fast halfway through the door which had swung open in the tree's base. The Widgets jerked the wheelbarrow free, turned it around and began to reverse frantically into the tree trunk—just as Scott and Amanda burst into the clearing.

'It's a Veeton!' yelled Scott, spotting the wheelbarrow.

But the barrow vanished into the tree, and the door slammed shut.

Word magic

Amanda rushed to the tree and tugged and pushed at the door, but it was firmly locked. Boris was all for bashing it down with his bat.

'There must be a key,' said Amanda. 'There's a keyhole.'

'We haven't got time to look for a key,' said Scott. He rather liked the idea of bashing down the door.

'Wait!' commanded Gorwen. 'Perhaps the Widgets have a key?' He had noticed two of the furry boxes of tricks watching nearby. What he *hadn't* noticed was one of the Widgets finding Rodey in the fallen leaves which carpeted the clearing. The Widgets had kangaroo-style pouches on their tummies for just such occasions—and the helpless mouse had been deftly plopped inside.

'Let's ask them,' agreed Amanda, then she remembered and looked around rather impatiently. 'Where's Rodey?'

'Still sulking somewhere,' said Scott. 'Come on, Boris.'

Boris laid his bat carefully on the ground and then clicked his fingers twice.

'Bat, length . . . and strength.'

Instantly the bat grew to battering ram proportions. Scott and Boris picked it up and prepared to charge.

'Hey, hang on,' insisted Amanda. 'Let me try this first.'

She had written a message to the Widgets in her notebook:

Have you got a key?

But they just looked blank, even when she mimed turning a key in a lock.

'It's no use,' she shrugged. 'They can't read.'

'Hmm . . .' murmured Gorwen.

'Ready, Scott—one, two, three!' Boris was keen to get on with the bashing. They charged the tree door and there was a loud splintering of wood, but the door remained shut. Only the end of Boris's bat was damaged.

'There must be a *key*,' persisted Amanda. '*Where's* Rodey?'

The Widgets knew the answer. And they weren't telling. But when Jenny rang from the Veetacore House, the search party got some unexpected advice. From Morris.

'Ask the tree,' he said.

Amanda thought Morris was right. It was worth a try. *Anything* was worth a try. She stood in front of the tree and addressed it, firmly but politely.

'Excuse me. Can you tell us how to open this door?'

Scott and Boris smirked at each other. Fancy talking to a tree. Then their mouths dropped open and their tonsils almost fell out.

'You must find the key,' replied the tree in a husky, slightly creaky voice, as if its roots and branches were moving as it spoke.

Amanda managed to speak again, but not as boldly as before.

'We've looked but we can't find it.'

'The key is a word. A word is the key.'

'You mean a sort of password?' asked Amanda slowly. Was the tree going to help them?

'I know a password,' Scott butted in excitedly: 'Open Sesame!'

The tree laughed wheezily. 'More than a password. A keyword . . .'

Amanda was baffled. 'Keyword?'

Scott looked at her. 'A word that means the same as key?' He thought for a moment. 'Bolt?'

Amanda thought of some words as well.

'Latch? Catch?'

'Lock?' tried Scott. '*Un*lock?'

And they heard the sound of a key turning.

'Unlock!' cried Scott excitedly, but the door didn't open. 'Another word, Amanda, quick!'

Amanda couldn't think of anything else to do with keys and locks. 'Please?' she said, hopefully.

Again they heard a key turning.

'Unlock! Please!' cried Scott and Amanda together.

And the door swung open.

'Thank you . . .' Amanda rushed forward, and the others joined her, peering into the darkness inside the tree.

'Is the Veeton there?' asked Gorwen, who was too big to see through the low doorway.

'I don't know,' said Boris, 'I can't see anything. It's too dark.'

'Right,' said Amanda, taking charge. 'Boris and I'll go in. Gorwen, you and Scott must look for Rodey. Come on.'

And before Boris—or even Gorwen— could argue, the orange Keeper found himself pulled inside the tree. The door shut swiftly behind them of its own accord and, the moment it was too late, Amanda realised she had plunged in too quickly.

'We forgot the Veetarod!'

'What now?' asked Boris uneasily. After his experience with the quagmire, he was afraid that the tree would turn out to be another Widge trap. The darkness smelt of earth, wood and worms. He didn't like it.

But then a sign lit up on the inside of the tree trunk. A ghostly, greenish sign, but a sign none the less.

'Look, Boris! The sign says "Book Room" that way.'

'What do we want a book room for?'

Amanda didn't know. But it was the only sign there was.

'We'll get lost in the dark . . .' quavered Boris. The Book Room sign was pointing down a tunnel arched with tree roots. Being inside a tree was bad enough for Boris without going down narrow, winding tunnels. Widge tunnels . . .

Then Amanda had an idea.

'I read in a story once,' she said, 'about this man who was going into a sort of maze. He tied one end of a ball of string to the door before he started. And unwound it as he went. Then, when he wanted to come back again, he just followed the string.'

'Very clever,' said Boris sarcastically, 'but *we* haven't got a ball of string.'

'No, but your jumper's coming undone.'

And before Boris could stop her, she began pulling a bright orange thread from its bottom edge. She continued to pull until she had enough to tie to the door handle.

'But this is my *favourite* jumper!' protested Boris.

'Go on . . . go on . . . that way . . .' ordered Amanda, turning him in a circle and pushing him gently towards the dimly-lit passageway.


Jenny would have been grateful for an extra jumper in the Veetacore House. She was getting very, *very* cold now. Morris had knitted her some gloves, but she still shivered as she huddled over the Book. Morris himself was sitting in his rocking chair with a rug over his knees and Frug on his shoulder, keeping his neck warm. Even Doris was cold now. Her fingers were too numb to hold the pencil as she tried to add to the drawings in Jenny's notebook.

'It's getting worse and worse in here, Doris,' said a worried Jenny. 'Something's wrong. I think we should tell Gorwen.'

Doris hesitated. 'No,' she said firmly. 'We can't keep bothering him. He's busy.'

'Rodey!' roared Gorwen, breathing smoke and even a little fire in his angry frustration.

Behind his back, the two Widgets mimicked Gorwen with thinks bubbles as they scrabbled showers of leaves and earth in all directions, helping to search for the missing mouse.

Far below the Widgets' mischievous feet, Boris thought he could hear music. Weird, Widge music, like the wind in a spider's web. He didn't like it any more than he liked the endless tunnel through the tree roots, or the ghostly, greenish Book Room signs, or the fact that his best jumper was now half unravelled. Then the tunnel reached a junction and two different signs lit up:

'Exit?' frowned Boris. 'That's a way out, isn't it?' He didn't notice that he'd actually *read* a word.

'Yes,' said Amanda, not noticing either, 'but we're not going out, we've got to get to this Book Room. I'm *sure* the tree's trying to help.' And she led the way to the right.

Within seconds, she was calling excitedly over her shoulder. 'Come on, Boris, we're here . . .'

Boris followed Amanda as she pushed aside a soft green curtain, and found himself in a large chamber, roofed with tree roots. It was a cosy space, well lit, with comfortable-looking mossy cushions everywhere.

Amanda was standing looking around in delight. 'It's a sort of huge book corner,' she exclaimed.

Boris didn't exactly know what a book corner was, but if it was a place which burst at the seams with books, then this place was certainly like one. There were books everywhere except on the ceiling. Shelves of them, rows of them, piles of them. Knee-deep.

'But where's the Veeton?' Boris raised the lid of a large wooden chest and started to look for it.

'Nothing but books,' he scoffed.

'And books can help you!'

Boris jumped back from the chest. The tree had started talking again. Its voice seemed to be all around them.

'Books and words are on your side . . .'

'You know about our quest for the lost Veetons?' asked Amanda.

'Oh yes,' replied the tree. 'Many things are against you, and you have very little time. Pelamar is in grave danger.'

'Can you help us?'

'Look!' commanded the tree.

Amanda looked. On the one bare patch of wall in the Book Room a square of light appeared and, as the weird, wind-in-a-spider's web music began again, words began to form in it. A riddle:

> *'Can you see a candle*
> *if the sun is bright?*
> *What fun are fireworks*
> *if the sky is light?*
> *Remember, Amanda,*
> *the sun hides the moon.*
> *You must work out this riddle.*
> *You must do it soon!'*

'I can't! I don't know what it means,' cried Amanda, suddenly feeling useless. She turned miserably to Boris. 'I wish Scott was here. He's good at clues and riddles and things.'

'Are these any help?' To her surprise, Boris was handing Amanda two books he'd seen in the chest. Books about astronomy, with a sun and a moon on their covers.

As Amanda began to look through the two books, Boris's eyes were drawn back to the chest. Some of the book covers really did look attractive. He hesitated, then reached out . . .

'That one looks good, doesn't it?'

Again Boris jumped back guiltily.

'We have many books in Widge,' continued the tree. 'Look . . . These are brand new ones—they haven't been unpacked yet. Go on . . .' It sounded rather amused. 'Put some in your rucksack. Please, help yourself. You'll enjoy those stories when you can read.'

'Oh . . . er, thank you very much. Thank you.' Boris smiled nervously and stuffed books, some loose, some wrapped, into his rucksack.

'You're welcome,' said the tree. 'Now help Amanda. Your time is running short.'

Amanda needed help. She had found no clues in the astronomy books and was staring hopelessly at the riddle on the wall again.

'I can't do it, Boris. I just can't . . .'

'Shush,' said Boris soothingly, as he crouched beside her. 'Just read the first bit, okay?'

Amanda did so:

> 'Can you see a candle
> if the sun is bright?
> What fun are fireworks
> if the sky is light?'

Boris was thinking hard, taking it step by step. 'Candles and fireworks—that's two things you can't see when there's a bright light. But they're both things that give light themselves, aren't they?'

'But where does that get us?' Amanda still didn't see.

Boris didn't either, but he kept going. 'Veetons give light, and like candles they glow . . .'

'Boris, you're brilliant!' Amanda had jumped to her feet. 'The Veeton must be here, but we can't see it because the light's too bright!'

'Oh . . .' muttered Boris, rather bewildered, as Amanda searched the walls for something like a light switch. She found a creeper hanging by the curtain entrance and pulled it. The Book Room went dark, except for a familiar glow.

'There it is!' cried Boris.

The Veeton was clearly visible now, a square slab of gold standing on a table, wedged in a row of books.

Amanda picked it up and held it tight. 'Fantastic, Boris! We've found the first Veeton.' She looked up and smiled gratefully into the darkness. 'Thank you, Book Tree.'


'Enough is enough!' Gorwen had his suspicions and it was time to put them to the test. He grabbed one of the Widgets as they tumbled and tittered in the leaves, and breathed smoke as he demanded, 'Where is our friend Rodey?'

'Gorwen, he doesn't understand what you're saying,' objected Scott.

'Then write it down,' said the dragon.

Scott shrugged and did as he was told, even though he was sure the Widgets couldn't read. Gorwen kept tight hold of the Widget as Scott wrote the question in his notebook:

_____
    Where is Rodey?
_____

The Widget slowly put both hands in his pouch and produced the missing mouse.

'You Widgets *can* read!' Scott grabbed Rodey and turned to Gorwen. 'They've been tricking us all along!'

Gorwen didn't share Scott's angry surprise. He nodded wisely and let his captive go.

'Widgets will be Widgets . . .' was all he said.

Down among the roots of the Book Tree, Boris and Amanda were winding in the jumper thread, eagerly heading back towards daylight with their precious load. A little too eagerly. The taut thread suddenly snapped and twanged out of sight like a piece of elastic.

'Which one did it go down?' cried

Amanda, darting forward. They were at a fork in the tunnel.

'I don't know, I didn't see,' said Boris miserably. 'What shall we do *now*?'

Amanda was taking the Veeton from the rucksack and holding it up like a lantern. Above the two forks of the tunnel was a road sign:

She read it and shrugged. 'Well, we *are* lost, so it's got to be found.'

'Right!' said Boris, grabbing up the rucksack and disappearing into the darkness.

He had gone only a few paces when Amanda heard an alarmed shout, as if Boris were falling.

'Boris?' She plunged after him and the ground disappeared beneath *her* feet as well.

It wasn't a long fall, more a short slide really, and it ended in bright sunshine. Boris, Amanda, rucksack and Veeton tumbled out from under the tree roots into a kind of steep-sided gravel pit.

'Well,' said Boris, rubbing his bruised bits, 'we found the way out.'

Amanda wasn't interested in bruises.

She pulled Boris's cap from his head.

'Call Doris,' she said excitedly. 'Tell her we've found the first Veeton!'

Boris pressed the code button. Nothing happened. He shook the videophone impatiently and Doris's face suddenly appeared on the screen.

'Doris! Guess what? Me and Amanda . . .'

But Doris wasn't paying attention. She was slowly turning to her right, a look of horror on her face, as a dark shadow fell across her . . .

## 5 Clues in the snow

'Charn . . . !' Doris's voice was a whisper of horror as she stared towards the doorway of the Veetacore House. Jenny turned and could have screamed, but her own voice seemed to have run away. No-one could have blamed it, for never in her worst nightmares had Jenny come face to face with such a creature as stood before her now. Its head seemed part animal's skull, part beak. What skin Jenny could see seemed that of a reptile, but its chest had no flesh; the creature's rib-cage was clearly visible. Yet this was no skeleton but a tall, powerful figure, standing proud despite its ugliness. The flowing black cloak seemed to slither as the creature moved towards them and that was when Jenny first saw its hands, or were they talons—or even gauntlets? Ending in long, fearsome fingers that were straight, hard and pointed. They looked like weapons.

'Doris. How lovely to see you again after so long . . .' The voice was a smooth hiss, cold and full of menace. The dangerous voice of a being that had no heart and was rather pleased about it.

Poor Morris seemed to be frozen in the act of lifting a Veeton from the floor. The creature nodded politely at him. 'Morris . . . But you both look so *cold* . . .'

Boris's face was still visible on the video screen. Unaware of what was happening, he was getting cross.

'Doris! What's the matter? I'm trying to talk to you. We've done it. We've found the first Veeton. Doris, are you listening?'

Doris's eyes darted from the creature to the video screen and she opened her mouth to speak.

'Oh, I wouldn't do that, Doris . . .' hissed the creature. 'Poor Boris would miss you so . . .' And green fire flickered at the ends of those terrible fingers.

Doris switched off the video.

'Of all the cheek,' exclaimed Boris, as his screen went blank. 'She's cut me off!'

In the Veetacore House the creature swirled its cloak and sneered. 'So, Boris has found a Veeton? Not on his *own*, I'm sure . . .' The skull beak turned sharply towards Jenny and the fingers pointed. 'And you are . . . ?'

Jenny's voice came out of hiding. Very small and dry. 'Jenny. I'm Jenny.'

'Ah yes. Jenny—from the other world . . . So pleased to meet you, Jenny. I am Charn.'

But there was no way Jenny could shake the hand that was thrust towards her.

'No?' laughed Charn. 'Well, never mind.' He turned. 'You'll shake hands with your old friend Charn, won't you, Morris?' Again the fingers flickered.

Morris, still clutching the Veeton he had picked up, backed away, speechless with terror.

'Oh come now . . . That's not a very nice way to welcome back a fellow Pelamot.'

'You're not a Pelamot any more, Charn,' cried Doris defiantly. 'You were banished long ago. You're evil!'

'*Me?*' exclaimed Charn, in mock amazement. He came close to Jenny, looming over her, the cruel beak inches from her face. 'Do I look *that* bad? They sent me away, you know. Threw me out . . . for nothing. I've been living in the cold, wet wastelands ever since. All alone, waiting . . . thinking about things . . .'

'What things?' Doris was still defiant.

'Oh . . . power. Getting my own back . . . Of course, it wasn't possible until the Veetacore exploded.'

'And now?' asked Doris.

'And now I shall be master of Pelamar.' Charn stretched his arms wide so that his swirling, slithering cloak seemed to fill the room. 'With your help the Veetacore will be mended in no time. You're doing very well. And when the last Veeton is in place, *I* shall chant the spell *my* way . . .'

Jenny glanced at Doris, scared and puzzled. 'The spell?'

'You don't *know* about the spell?' Charn was surprised.

Jenny shook her head.

'It's inside the back cover of the Book, I believe,' said Charn. 'Not that *I* can read, of course . . . but I do have a very good memory. Don't I, Doris?' He turned sharply to Jenny. 'Look it up.'

Jenny did so. The spell was there, inside the back cover:

> 'Power of good
> spread near and far.
> Power of good
> give life to Pelamar.
>
> Banish evil thoughts,
> banish evil ways.
> Make a world full of good
> from the Veetacore's rays.'

As she finished reading aloud, Jenny looked up with a frown. 'But what's it for?'

'The spell must be chanted as we fit the last Veeton,' sighed Doris. 'But if *he* says the wrong words . . .'

Charn began to chant with great relish:

> 'Power of *evil*
> spread near and far.
> Power of *evil*
> bring *death* to Pelamar . . .'

Then he laughed. 'All Pelamots will grow cruel and wicked and I, Charn, shall rule!' And again he swept his cloaked arms wide.

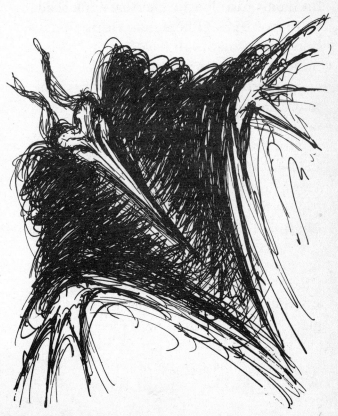

'No.' Jenny was shaking, but her voice was firm and brave. Doris and Morris looked up, startled. Charn slowly lowered his arms.

'I think it would be better to let Pelamar fade away,' went on Jenny quietly, but still looking straight at Charn. She closed the Book. 'I won't help you mend the Veetacore.'

There was a silence. Doris and Morris held their breath. Then Charn began to clap his hands in a slow mockery of applause.

'Bravo! Did you hear that, Doris? What a brave little friend you have.'

Doris's defiance had come back, encouraged by Jenny's example. 'Yes,' she said. 'And *you* need her just as much as we do.'

'Oh, I do realise that . . . *Jenny* can read the Book. *Jenny* must be kept safe at all costs . . .' He looked ominously around the room. 'But we don't need that ridiculous caterpillar, do we?'

Morris realised what was about to happen—too late. Green fire flashed from Charn's fingertips and instantly the giant caterpillar shrivelled and disappeared. In its place on the tablecloth lay a green puddle.

'Frug!' cried Morris, in helpless dismay.

'Now . . .' hissed Charn, 'who else don't we need?' and he stretched those deadly fingers towards Morris himself.

'No!' cried Jenny.

With his fingers still poised, Charn turned slowly and looked down at her. 'Then you *will* help?'

Jenny nodded.


It was a sunny afternoon in Widge and the search party had been re-united. The Veetarod had led Gorwen and Scott to the gravel pit, and Boris, forgetting his annoyance with Doris, had launched himself into an excited account of the finding of the first Veeton.

'You have been very brave, Boris,' said Gorwen, cutting him off as politely as he could. 'But there are still two more Veetons to be found. Where next?'

'Can't the Veetarod help us?' asked Amanda.

'Not until we get close to the next Veeton,' said Gorwen.

Boris looked up suddenly. 'Wonderful Widge . . .' he groaned. 'It's started to snow.'

A few large snowflakes were indeed floating down. Scott and Amanda were both delighted.

'Quick, catch them!' cried Amanda,

holding out her hands. But when she looked closer at the snowflake pattern on her palm, she was amazed.

'A.J.—my initials. Amanda Jackson . . .'

Scott had caught one too. 'S.B.—that's me! Scott Bates!'

'B for Boris.' Amanda was peering at the Keeper's hand now. 'This is great!'

'Yeah,' said Scott, a thought striking him. 'Maybe it's a clue!'

He whipped off his black jerkin and spread it on the ground, and, as they all watched, snowflake letters settled on it in the form of a kind of crossword puzzle, without the clues:

```
R ❋ ❋ N ❋
O F ❋ O ❋
C ❋ ❋ R ❋
K ❋ ❋ T O
❋ A S H ❋
```

'Words again,' said Amanda. 'The Tree said words would help us. Quick, let's write it down before it melts!'

'Of . . . to . . . Ash . . . Rock . . . north.' Scott read the words aloud and Amanda wrote them in her notebook.

'North? I bet it's telling us where to go next!' Scott's mind was racing ahead. 'Ash Rock. Is that a place?'

It was indeed. Clearly marked on the map

of Widge. As was the gravel pit in which they now crouched. Ash Rock was to the north.

'North . . . to . . . Ash . . . Rock . . . That's it!' said Scott, sure that he'd solved the snowflake clue.

'But what about the "of"?' frowned Amanda. 'It could be "North *of* Ash Rock".'

'Let's just *go* there then,' said Boris, getting up rather impatiently, 'before it *really* starts to snow.'

'Ow!' There was a muffled squeak from Scott's pocket as Amanda picked up the jerkin.

'Rodey,' said Scott, 'I forgot about you.'

'*I'll* look after him,' smiled Amanda, glad the mouse was back with them again. And she slipped him into her peppermint pocket.

'What happened to your jumper, Boris?' laughed Scott.

The orange Keeper didn't reply. He just stumped off with his nose in the air.

Soon they had left the trees behind and were trudging north across a broad, flat plain. There was already a thick covering of snow on the ground.

'Just like Widge,' grunted Boris. 'Hot and sunny one minute, snowy the next.'

As he spoke a snowball whacked him on the head and knocked his cap flying.

'It's the Widgets!' cried Amanda, as snowballs began to whizz at them from all directions.

'Right!' yelled Boris, dropping his bat and rucksack. 'Are we just going to take this?'

'No way!' Scott was already scooping up a handful of snow.

Boris's cap lay unnoticed where it had fallen, and nobody saw Doris's fearful, wary face on its video screen.

'Boris?' she whispered. 'Tell Gorwen Charn is . . .'

That was all. Doris's face seemed to freeze, then the screen was awash with purple . . .

In the Veetacore House, Jenny gazed white-faced with shock at the purple puddle dripping onto the floor by the video screen. Charn advanced towards it, his fingers still pointing at the pair of glasses floating in the middle of the puddle.

'You always were hot-headed, Doris . . .' he hissed. Then he turned to Jenny. 'You won't try to contact Gorwen again, will you . . . I have excellent eyesight . . . and hearing.'

Jenny shook her head. But she was thinking, thinking furiously.

'Good,' snapped Charn. 'Read on.'

'Please, Charn,' trembled Jenny, 'I'm so cold . . . Will you let Morris knit a scarf for me?'

Charn looked at her suspiciously. 'A scarf?'

'Yes. I'll draw a pattern. It won't take long.'

Jenny stared at the long, flexing fingers, half expecting them to flash at her at any moment. She tried not to imagine what it would feel like to be melted. What colour puddle would *she* be? Pale pink, she supposed.

'Very well,' hissed Charn. 'But no tricks.'

Morris was huddled in his chair, shocked, terrified and cold. He wasn't in the mood for fancy knitting. But something in Jenny's look made him pay attention as she started to mark out a pattern in her notebook.

'There, Morris. Knit me a scarf. Look, like this . . .'

Even Gorwen was enjoying the snowball fight. Amanda certainly was. But as she turned to scoop up more snow, her laughter changed to surprised anger.

'Hey! Hey you, stop!'

A Widget had grabbed Boris's rucksack and was running off with it. In the rucksack was the Veeton.

Amanda sprinted after him. There wasn't time to tell the others. While she slipped and stumbled, the Widget padded rapidly on, his short tail bobbing, his cheeky face glancing occasionally at her over his shoulder.

The other Widgets seemed to have had enough of the snowball fight and started to retreat beyond a snowdrift.

'Whoopee!' yelled Boris. 'We've got them on the run!'

'Where's Amanda?' Scott's worried voice made the others turn. 'And where's the Veeton?'

Boris's bat and cap still lay in the snow, but nothing else. Just two sets of footprints.

'One Widget and Amanda . . .' said Gorwen. He considered briefly, then looked at Scott. 'You and Boris go on to Ash Rock, and wait there. *I* will find Amanda and the rucksack.' Scott protested but Gorwen pushed him gently on his way with Boris, then turned to follow the footprints.

The Widget seemed to have led Amanda quite a dance across the snowy landscape. Over snowdrifts, down into dips, round in circles. Then the footprints petered out close to another notice board. The memory of Boris's adventure with the quagmire made Gorwen stop.

'Oh dear. Words again . . .' He knew the notice didn't say 'Danger! Quagmire!' but what *did* it say? He thought the second word began with 'i', so he looked around for clues. There was ice in front of him.

'Ice?' he muttered to himself. 'Could be ice. "Something" ice . . . What kind of ice?' He grunted as he stooped to dig a stone out of the snow with his claw.

Gorwen threw the stone, and the ice in front of him cracked and splintered. Deadly cold water showed through from below.

'Thin ice!' Gorwen checked the notice board. Yes, he was pretty sure the first word began with 'th' . . .

'Definitely "Thin ice",' he nodded.

'Thank you for the warning. I like "Thin ice" better than "Gorwen's grave" . . .'

Far ahead of Gorwen, Amanda was still chasing through the snow. She was exhausted. The only thing that kept her going was the fact that the Widget was obviously tiring too. Then at last he lost his footing and Amanda got within reach.

'Got you!' she cried, grabbing at the rucksack, as the Widget went down in a flurry of snow and furry limbs. The Widget squeaked and struggled, but Amanda held on tight. In the end he left her to it, letting go of the rucksack and hurrying off, while she looked anxiously inside to make sure the Veeton was still there. It was, but Amanda's relief was short-lived. Here she was, alone, without shelter, miles from anywhere. She looked up at the sky. It was darkening again. That ominous grey-yellow colour that means more snow. The new flakes fell gently at first, but soon the blizzard had begun in earnest and whichever way Amanda turned, she seemed to be surrounded by a dense wall of whiteness.

'Come on, Amanda Jackson. You're not a baby.' There was a small spade in the rucksack and, muttering to herself as she did so, Amanda began to dig into the nearest snowdrift with it, scooping out a hollow in which she could shelter from the storm.

As she worked, she became aware of a muffled voice, somewhere nearby. For a moment she thought the others had found her, then she realised her pocket was alive.

'Amanda! Quick! Let me out! Let me out!'

'Rodey!' cried Amanda, 'I'd forgotten about you.'

The mouse sat on the palm of her hand, panting slightly.

'I think I can grow again,' he squeaked excitedly. 'I feel stronger. Put me down, please.'

Amanda did so and Rodey's tiny paws had barely touched the snow before he began to shimmer at her feet. He seemed to spin and swirl and swell. Then he was standing, looking her in the eye, ruffled and out of breath but full Pelamot size once again.

'Typical Widge weather,' grunted Boris. 'Snow one minute, sunshine the next.'

He and Scott were crossing a barren field towards a large, solitary boulder, shaped rather like an upended grey box. The snow had all but disappeared and in the distance they could see the steep, jagged, jumbled mountains quite clearly.

'Suppose this is it then? Ash Rock?' Boris looked from the boulder to Scott, who was studying the map.

'Must be,' said Scott, walking slowly round the boulder. 'There's nothing here. Well, if it wasn't north *to* Ash Rock, then it must have been north *of* Ash Rock.' He looked at the map again and moved his finger in a straight line from the gravel pit to Ash Rock and beyond. 'No . . . *to* the north *of* Ash Rock. Straight on.'

Boris held out the Veetarod in the direction Scott was indicating and it trembled slightly.

'Yeah, looks like it,' he said. 'Come on then, what are we waiting for?'

'Gorwen and Amanda,' said Scott. 'Gorwen said we had to stay here.'

Boris didn't want to wait, and if he *had* to wait he wanted to play cricket. Scott wanted to write in his notebook first. So he gave Boris a comic. Boris gave *him* a look and a sigh. But when Scott had finished writing and was ready to play, Boris's nose was still well and truly stuck in the comic. He didn't want to move, and when he did, he banged himself painfully against the Rock.

'Ow! This thing's sharp.'

Scott peered more closely at the Rock, then started running his hands over its surface.

'Hey, Boris! I think words are going to help us again. Have you got a piece of paper, a big sheet?'

Actually, Boris did have. In his pocket was some wrapping paper—he'd undone one of the bundles from the Book Tree. The Book Tree . . . He had a faraway look in his eyes as he handed the paper over.

'Great!' said Scott. 'Hold it tight and don't let it slip.'

He pressed the paper against the Rock and a puzzled Boris did as he was told, holding it in place as Scott took a crayon from his pocket and began to rub the surface of the paper with it. Slowly but surely, words began to appear through the crayon shading, just like they do in a brass rubbing.

'It's working!' cried Scott. Then, as Boris's cap phone began to ring, 'Don't answer that. Don't move until I've finished.'

'But it might be important.' Leaning his arm against the paper to hold it in place, Boris managed to remove his cap.

'What do you want me to say?' asked Jenny. She was glancing anxiously at Charn as the interference on the Veetacore House video screen began to clear.

'Just ask how they're getting on,' hissed Charn. 'But remember, I'm listening . . .' And a warning flicker of deadly green fire danced from his fingertips towards Morris.

'Hi. So you *do* want to talk to us.' Boris's lopsided face beamed up at Jenny from the screen. 'Where's Doris?'

Jenny's eyes slid towards the glasses and purple puddle on the floor. 'Er . . . She's not here at the moment . . . She's . . .'

'She's fine,' hissed Charn.

'She's fine.'

'Well, tell her we've found the first Veeton,' said Boris, 'but now we've lost it again.'

Charn raised his arms in silent frustration. Boris couldn't see him, but he could see something else. Pink and turquoise puddles on the workbench.

'What are all those puddles?'

Jenny was startled. 'Oh, uh . . .' She darted a desperate look at Charn. 'We had a bit of an accident . . .'

Charn nodded approvingly.

'Boris! You're letting the paper slip again.' Jenny could hear Scott's voice. She longed to shriek her message to him, but when Boris sighed 'All right, I'd better go. Anything else?' all she said was 'No. Bye. . .'

'I wonder where Doris is?' frowned Boris, putting his cap back on. 'You finished yet?'

'Nearly. Can you keep your end still!' Scott was getting cross. 'There . . . Hold it up, will you.'

Boris lifted the paper away from the Rock and held it by the top corners, looking down at it. He giggled.

'Writing's even funnier upside down.'

'There's nothing funny about this,' said Scott, studying what seemed to be a sort of poem. The only trouble was, there were a lot of gaps:

TO GET TO THE

YOU MUST GO TO THE BOTTOM.

B          OF

THAT FALL FROM THE AIR.

BE        E OF A FLOOR

THAT IS NOT THERE.

THEN CLIMB ON        AGAIN.

'That's supposed to help, is it?' grunted Boris scornfully, when Scott had read it aloud for him.

'It's a clue,' said Scott. 'We must work it out, like the crossword.' He pondered the first bit. 'To get to the "something" you must go to the bottom . . . Remember that for now, will you. We'll work it out as we go north.' And he briskly folded the paper and stood up.

'What about Gorwen and Amanda?' asked Boris. 'We're supposed to wait for them.'

'That was before we found this,' said Scott, smoothing the paper flat.

'We should at least leave a sign or something, to show which way we've gone,' persisted Boris, being unusually sensible.

'Give me some of your pens.'

Scott took a handful of coloured pens from his pocket and Boris arranged them on the ground beside the Rock: three in the shape of an arrow, three more in the shape of a capital N.

'"N" for North?' smiled Boris, looking up at Scott. He knew he was right and was rather pleased with himself.


'Amanda . . . Amanda . . .' Gorwen was still plodding across a totally white landscape. The blizzard had stopped but the going was still deep and difficult, with treacherous snowdrifts all around.

'Amanda . . .' His strong voice had grown hoarse from calling her name a thousand times.

One of the snowdrifts seemed to answer, 'Gorwen . . .' And then it erupted and out burst Amanda herself. 'Gorwen!'

She threw her arms around the dragon and hugged him tight, feeling his smoky breath so warm and comforting on her back. Then she turned excitedly to the hollow in the snow.

'Look! Rodey's grown big again.'

'And we've got this,' said the mouse, proudly holding up the first Veeton.

Scott wasn't too keen on heights. So, as he and Boris walked along the narrow, curving mountain path, he was careful not to look to his left. Because there was nothing there. Just thin air and a very long drop. On his right, the side of the mountain rose vertically into the clouds. Boris was striding on ahead with the Veetarod.

'Hey, we must be nearing a Veeton—look at the shake on this!'

'Let's have a rest,' sighed Scott, 'I'm exhausted.' And he leaned against a wooden gate across the path. He *was* hot and tired but he was also feeling wobbly because of the narrowness of the path and the steepness of the drop. He wasn't going to admit that to Boris, though. The orange Keeper had clambered over the gate and was waiting rather impatiently.

'Well, I've worked it out,' said Scott. 'The clue from Ash Rock. Just the first bit: To get to the "something" you must go to the bottom . . . The missing word must be "top".'

'Why?'

'It's like a riddle. Top's the opposite of bottom. And you've got to go to the bottom of a mountain before you can get to the top.'

'Right,' nodded Boris. 'So we must be on the right track. *Up* we go, if you're not too exhausted. Race you to that notice board!'

And while Scott was still climbing over the gate, Boris ran off. 'Last one reads what it says!' he shouted, touching the board before Scott could get close.

Scott looked at the notice board hanging amongst the foliage on the right of the path, and shrugged.

'It says "Road Safe".'

'That's all right then,' said Boris, marching briskly on. Scott hesitated for a puzzled moment, then followed. When they were out of sight, a furry paw removed a large leaf which had fallen across the notice board, and voices in the foliage tittered quietly. 'Road Safe' was really 'Road *Un*safe' . . .

The Veetarod was now trembling more violently than ever.

'We *must* be near a Veeton,' cried Boris, still ahead of Scott. 'What's the next bit of the clue?'

Scott read from the crayoned paper. '"B-something" of "something" that fall from the air.'

But as he spoke there was a brief rumbling and an avalanche of rocks slid from the cliff above. Scott jumped back, but Boris was trapped. A golden sphere cracked him on the head and he fell to the ground as other rocks bounced around him. Then all was quiet.

Scared for himself, and for Boris, Scott crept warily forward, glancing up at the cliff as he went. 'Boris?' He knelt beside the fallen Pelamot, his voice a frightened whisper. 'Boris . . . ?'

How long Scott was there, crouching beside the orange Keeper on that mountain path, he never knew. Boris was too heavy to move and, in any case, moving him might have started another avalanche. He tried contacting Gorwen on the cap phone, but the cap was buckled and bent and wouldn't work. Then he heard a powerful, familiar voice echoing around the mountains:

'Boris . . . Boris . . . Boris . . . !'

And, forgetting his fear of avalanches,
Scott leapt to his feet and yelled back,
'Gorwen!'

Soon Amanda was crouching with Scott
beside Boris, while Gorwen and Rodey
looked anxiously on. The Keeper groaned
and opened one eye.

'Ooh . . . my head . . .' He struggled to sit
up. 'It must have rained rocks.'

'Yeah, but look,' grinned Scott, 'this one
hit you on the head.'

Amanda presented Boris with the glowing
golden sphere.

'Oh!' exclaimed the Keeper proudly. 'I've found another Veeton!'

'The hard way, of course,' laughed Amanda.

But their celebrations were cut short by more ominous rumblings above.

'The mountain . . .' said Gorwen. 'This is not a safe place. We must move at once!'

And while Amanda and Scott gathered up rucksack, cricket bat and cap, Gorwen and Rodey helped Boris along the path.

'Didn't you see the notice?' asked Amanda. 'Road Unsafe?'

'*Un*safe?' Scott looked at her. There was no need to guess who'd changed it. The Widgets!

'Who's got the Veetarod?' asked Amanda, suddenly realising that it was missing. And before Scott could stop her, she was darting away down the path to pick it up.

'Amanda!' Scott's voice was lost in the roar of the mountain as rocks began to fall, the heaviest of all crashing onto the path a split second after Amanda had plucked up the Veetarod and fled. And as Scott escaped too, he was sure he heard the mountain laugh. A cracking, booming laugh that rolled along the cliff face behind them . . .

At last the search party found a safe place to rest: a broad, flat ledge of rock, well away from the crumbling cliff face. Scott had found a seemingly endless bandage in Boris's seemingly bottomless rucksack, and while he and Rodey wound it round and round the Keeper's head, Amanda tried to straighten out the cap phone.

Boris was rather edgy. 'Any luck?' he asked. 'I want to know where Doris is.'

Gorwen looked up. 'Doris? Why?'

'Well, she wasn't there when Jenny called earlier.'

'How are they getting on?' asked Amanda.

Boris frowned. 'I don't really know. Jenny was a bit . . . funny. And there were all these puddles. All over the place . . .' His voice trailed away, as if his words dimly reminded him of something, though he wasn't sure what.

'Puddles?' said Amanda.

'Yes . . . And they were all different colours . . .'

Amanda could sense a change in the three Pelamots. They were looking at each other, sharing some kind of unspoken worry. Gorwen unhooked his videophone and pressed the Veetacore House code button.

Morris was just finishing Jenny's scarf when Gorwen's face appeared on the screen.

'Good news, Jenny. We now have two Veetons.'

'Oh. Good.' Jenny was so tense she could hardly speak.

'You look unwell,' said Gorwen. 'Is there anything wrong?'

'No. I'm fine. Just a bit cold, that's all . . .' She glanced at Charn, standing poised and watchful as ever, and took a quick breath in case her voice gave out on her. It had to be now.

'Morris is kindly knitting a scarf for me,' she said. 'I'll show you.' She took the scarf from Morris and held it up in front of the video screen. 'My new scarf. What do you think?'

Jenny could see Scott and Amanda peering over Gorwen's shoulder. She held the scarf up long enough for them to read the message knitted into it:

**HELP! CHARN!**

They *had* to read it. But if either of them read it aloud . . . If either of them asked her what it meant . . . She could hear Charn's fingertips clattering restlessly.

'It's lovely.' Amanda's voice was puzzled

101

but wary. 'The pattern's brilliant. Did *you* make it up?'

'Yes,' said Jenny. Then, glancing at Charn and dropping the scarf, 'I've got to go now. I'm glad you like it. Bye . . .'

There was a moment's silence on the mountainside as Scott and Amanda gazed at the blank screen.

'It was a message, wasn't it?' asked Gorwen, in a voice that suggested he already knew the answer.

Amanda looked at the Pelamots. She was becoming worried too. 'Help. Charn . . .'

Both Rodey and Boris reacted in terror at the name, instinctively flinching and backing away as if green fire was flickering from Amanda's lips. But Gorwen was already preparing to move.

'I must return at once to Pelamar,' he said grimly. 'Alone. Boris, find me something to carry the Veetons in. I will take them with me. You must find the last one on your own.'

'Oh, Gorwen . . .' quailed Rodey.

'There is no time to lose!' The dragon had clearly made up his mind.

Boris quickly rummaged in his rucksack, found a shoe-bag and tipped out several pairs of old trainers. Rodey replaced them with the two Veetons, while Scott and

Amanda looked on in frightened bewilderment.

'What's happened?' asked Scott. 'Why do you have to go?'

'What's Charn?' asked Amanda.

Gorwen stood erect. 'Charn is the enemy of Pelamar. I have defeated him in the past . . . And now I must face him once again.'

'Gorwen, not on your own!' cried Amanda, sensing great danger for the dragon, and she rushed forward, trying to stop him.

But both Rodey and Boris seemed to have accepted it all.

'No one else can face Charn and live,' said Rodey, pulling her gently away.

'No,' said Boris. 'Only Gorwen has a chance . . .'

So as Gorwen carried the Veetons away and disappeared back down the mountain path, there was nothing Amanda could do but wave a tearful farewell.

# 7 The waterfall of words

Gorwen strode quickly through the woods. He had left the mountains behind now, and Ash Rock. It was his plan to get past the quagmire before nightfall, but already stars were beginning to appear and around him in the darkening trees owls were calling—or was it Widgets? Certainly he knew he was being watched every step of the way, but no trick or trap that Widge could surprise him with now was of any importance. Not compared with the challenge he must face in Pelamar . . .

The rest of the search party had pitched camp for the night. Naturally enough, Boris had a tent in his rucksack. It was cosy inside but a bit of a squash, especially when Scott spread out the wrapping paper clue in front of him.

```
B               OF
THAT  FALL  FROM  THE  AIR.
BE          E OF A FLOOR
THAT  IS  NOT  THERE.
THEN  CLIMB  ON        AGAIN.
```

Amanda studied it. 'Be "something-e" of a floor that is not there . . . Sounds dangerous.'

'Be . . . careful?' tried Scott.

'Careful doesn't end in "e".'

Scott thought again. 'Uh . . . be . . . be . . . beware!'

'Yeah!' cried Amanda. 'Beware, beware. *Two* warnings.' She grinned at Boris. 'Well, we know what the first one was, don't we. Beware of rocks that fall from the air.' And she and Scott both laughed.

'It wasn't a rock,' said Boris, very loftily, 'it was a Veeton.' And, giving them both a look, he buried his face in his sleeping bag.

Scott filled in the words they'd worked out, then frowned again. 'What about the next bit? Beware of a floor that is not there. Then climb on "something" again. Climb on in? Climb on out? Down? Up?'

'Up!' said Amanda. 'It's got to be up. To get to the top of the mountain.'

Scott filled in the clue's last blank space.

'Let's look at the map,' said Amanda eagerly. But they couldn't. Boris was sleeping on it. So there was nothing else to do except get some rest themselves. Though whether they would have fallen asleep so peacefully if they had noticed the tent flap being slowly unzipped is another matter . . .

Gorwen could smell the quagmire before he could actually see it. He could hear it too, bubbling hopefully, as if it had been woken by his approaching footsteps. The log was still there, but Gorwen hesitated before stepping onto it. If he were to slip . . . Then he imagined that Charn was standing on dry land on the other side of the quagmire, waiting for him, and he strode firmly across.

It wasn't so much the early morning sunshine that woke Boris as the throbbing inside his head. But as he opened his eyes, he became aware of something else. A wheezing, whistling sound. Not the kind of sound Scott or Amanda would make. No, more the kind of sound you'd get from a pile of snoozing Widgets . . . Boris sat up rapidly.

'Oi!'

Three Widgets, packed like comfortable sardines just inside the tent flap, woke with a startled squeak, unzipped the tent and tumbled out as Boris dived after them.

'I'll give you Road *Safe*!' But the squeaking, tittering Widgets were much too quick for him.

106

'They haven't done any harm,' said Amanda, woken up by the noise and confusion.

'You're not inside my head.'

Amanda grinned at Boris. 'Sometimes I wonder what is.'

Normally Amanda would have enjoyed sitting outside a tent on a mountainside on a fine blue morning, but it was hard not to wonder what was going to happen back in Pelamar.

'Gorwen will beat Charn, won't he?' she asked, as she unpacked breakfast from the rucksack later on.

'It depends how weak he is without the Veetacore,' said Boris grimly. 'He needs it as much as the rest of us. And Charn knows it.'

The silence that followed was broken by Rodey coming out of the tent.

'Isn't breakfast ready yet?' he asked grumpily.

'Whenever you like,' said Amanda. 'It's only milk and biscuits.'

'Ugh!' squeaked the mouse. 'I'll find my own.' And off he marched towards a clump of trees.

Amanda got up quickly to follow. 'I'd better go with him—he might shrink again. Don't spill any milk on the map.'

Scott absently picked up the map and put

it on a rock behind him. 'What sort of
biscuits are they?' he asked, as Boris
emptied the tin onto the picnic rug.

'Broken biscuits,' smiled Boris, studying
them. 'Some have got words on them. Some
haven't.'

Scott looked at him in surprise. 'What's
that bit say?' he asked, pointing at a broken
half.

Boris peered at it. 'Sh . . . short?'

'Well done,' grinned Scott. 'Here's the
other bit.' And he fitted the second half of
the biscuit against the first. 'Short . . .'

'. . . cake!' exclaimed Boris. 'That's clever.'
Soon he had found and fitted 'Ginger' and
'nut', but he had more trouble with the
next one.

'Whole,' said Scott.

'Whole?' Boris knew what should go with
it and pounced on a fragment of biscuit.
'Wholemeal! But that's not a "whole meal"
for me, is it?' he grinned.

'Boris!' groaned Scott. 'We call old jokes
like that "chestnuts".'

'Do you? We call them "cornflakes".'

Scott groaned again and they both
laughed, while behind their backs a familiar
furry paw removed the map from the rock.

Scott turned and frowned. 'Uh, Boris, did
you take the map?'

Boris hadn't taken it, but he was just realising who had. 'Scott,' he said quietly, 'over there. Look!'

Scott looked towards the mountain path. A Widget was peeping out from behind a rock, waving a folded piece of paper at him.

'Oi you! That's our map!' yelled Scott, springing up and giving chase.

Amanda and Rodey were picking Widge-fruit as the Widget with the map came crashing and squeaking through the undergrowth behind them. Scott was in hot pursuit. 'Amanda! After him, Amanda, quick!'

Beyond the trees was a large clearing, close against the steep mountainside, and on a ledge, just out of reach, sat a Widget. He squeaked and chippered with delight as his partner in crime, the map stuffed in his pouch, scrambled up to join him. Then they produced large pea-shooter-like tubes, and thinks bubbles appeared above their heads:

And as Scott appeared in the clearing, an acorn whacked him on the cheek.

Rodey and Amanda got the same

treatment as they arrived, but at last the
Widgets stopped the bombardment and
Scott was able to step forward.

'Give us back our map,' he demanded,
thrusting out his hand. 'Now!'

The Widgets looked at each other. The
one with the map tore it solemnly in two
and gave half to his friend. Then the two of
them proceeded to rip their halves into tiny
pieces, squeaking with joyful excitement as
they did so, and finished by tossing the
scraps of paper into the air with a flourish.

'Got the map back yet?' asked Boris
brightly, as he entered the clearing.

Gorwen flew slowly. He had reached the Border Camp without mishap, but the long flight home was draining his strength. Never before had he felt as weary as he did now. The familiar landscape of Pelamar far below brought him no joy or encouragement either. It seemed to have faded visibly even in the short time he had been away. And there on the distant horizon was the Veetacore House itself, the heart of Pelamar, and of its problems. Had Charn got wind of his coming? Gorwen flew on and hoped against hope that he had not . . .

'We've got no map, no time . . .'

'And no words to help us. Wonderful.'

Both Scott and Boris were utterly fed up. And Amanda and Rodey weren't feeling any better. The four of them were just sitting in the clearing, at a loss about what to do next, where to go, anything . . . Until a familiar sound made Amanda slowly look up. Not *that* familiar, she'd only heard it once before, but she would never forget it. A kind of silvery splashing sound, like magical water tinkling over a waterfall. A waterfall! She turned and stared.

'No words, Boris?' she whispered.

The others were staring too. Because

where, only seconds before, had been the bare earth and rocks of a dried-up watercourse, was now a shimmering curtain of light, cascading down the mountainside. Carrying the lines of a poem with it . . .

Boris sat quite still, watching raptly as each line of words appeared, shimmered down and slid away. He felt a sudden desire, a will, to be able to read, to play a full part in this quest for which these children from the other world were prepared to risk their lives. And when the poem appeared for a second time, Scott and Amanda were surprised to hear Boris reading it aloud with them. So they left him to it. A few of the words he already knew. Some he could work out. The rest? Boris somehow *knew* that word-magic was on his side as he read:

> 'The uphill climb
> will take much time.
> If you must be quick,
> find the arch of brick.
> Go in, if you dare!
> Beware! Beware!'

Rodey was staring at him in amazement. 'Boris! You can read that?' He sounded a tiny bit jealous.

'The arch of brick . . . Where's that?' asked Amanda.

'I don't know . . .' Scott's eyes were still fixed on the mesmerising waterfall.

Rodey jumped up and turned busily away. 'Well, I suggest we start looking for it.'

As Rodey moved, the spell seemed to be broken. The poem tumbled off the bottom of the fall and the magical water quickly followed. Only rocks and bare, dry earth remained . . .

'Come on, Morris. You can work faster than that,' hissed Charn impatiently.

Morris was heaving a large Veeton into place. When it was in position, one half of the Veetacore looked almost complete, its hexagonal outline unbroken. Jenny and Morris had been working hard. But of course the whole thing wasn't complete, nor could it be, even when every Veeton in the room had been fitted. And no amount of threats or puddles could make it so. Charn was well aware of this and it made his temper difficult to control.

'What's next?' he snapped at Jenny.

'I'm not sure. I need to look in the Book.' Jenny fumbled the pages over. She was numb with cold, despite wearing gloves and a scarf—*the* scarf. 'I can't understand the next bit,' she said.

'Really?' Charn flexed his fingers at Morris. 'You don't think she's not understanding on purpose? Wasting time? That wouldn't be wise, would it?'

Morris shook his head, terrified.

'I can hardly see to read any more,' said Jenny, looking at Charn. 'I need to be by the light.'

It was a reasonable request. The Veetacore House was becoming increasingly gloomy. Charn didn't object as Jenny crossed to a window with the Book and opened a shutter slightly. But as Jenny held the Book towards the daylight and leant forward to study the page, something outside caught her eye. Gorwen. Gorwen was there! Relief and panic fought inside Jenny as she stifled a shout. She tried not to stare. Tried to concentrate on the Book. But the words made even less sense than before.

'Come on . . .' hissed Charn.

Panic was gaining the upper hand inside Jenny. 'Yeah . . .' she blurted, 'the next bit says "the Veetons for . . ."'

Charn's patience snapped. He strode menacingly across to Jenny.

'I'm getting tired of wasting time,' he snarled.

There was nothing Jenny could do to keep him away from the window. But when he saw Gorwen, he became icily calm.

'Oh, we *have* been clever, haven't we?' he whispered.

Jenny tried to scream a warning, but the terrible fingers were suddenly clamped tight over her mouth.

'But not quite clever enough . . .'

Charn flexed the fingers of his free hand and his voice was almost musical in its quiet, deadly menace. 'Come, Gorwen . . . just a few steps closer and I've got you . . .'

# 8 The great battle

Morris had never thought of himself as a hero. But as he stood beside the Veetacore, watching Charn prepare to destroy Gorwen, he knew he must do *something*. Jenny was helpless. Doris was a puddle. If Gorwen became one as well, then nothing could stop Charn becoming master of Pelamar. Morris made up his mind and moved stealthily away towards the back door of the Veetacore House. With every step he expected to hear that deadly crackle which meant green fire flashing towards him. But nothing happened. Charn was too engrossed in savouring what was to come. Gorwen was almost within range . . .

Outside, Morris moved carefully round towards the front of the Veetacore House. He could see Gorwen now. The dragon had paused for a moment, looking towards the House as if unsure of what his next move should be. Morris paused too, then found himself running towards Gorwen. But as he left the sheltering wall of the House, he heard the window shutters open behind him and for a moment he lost his nerve. He dived for cover behind a fallen tree.

'Gorwen, my friend!' Charn's voice rang out, triumphant and cruel. He stood there, framed in the open window, Jenny still clasped tightly beside him, his free arm shooting forward, fingers outstretched.

'No!' Morris heard himself shout. He felt himself leap up. Then nothing but swirling, suffocating greenness. Like drowning in a whirlpool that swept you round in smaller and smaller circles, faster and faster, down and down towards some invisible plug-hole . . .

Gorwen had been slow to step back as Charn suddenly appeared, and the fizzing bolt of fiery green lightning would surely have hit him if Morris hadn't put himself deliberately in the way. Now there was just a green puddle behind the fallen tree, but Gorwen was still alive. He moved quickly, raising his wing to shield himself.

'Curse you, Morris!' Charn was furious. Pushing Jenny aside, he swirled over the low window-sill, hot for battle and confident of victory.

Gorwen breathed fire and his voice rumbled like a volcano preparing to erupt. 'Just you and me now, Charn. I should never have let you go . . .'

'Of course you shouldn't!' laughed Charn. And the outstretched fingers of both terrible hands flashed green lightning at the dragon.

The shielding wings were still strong, but for how long? Again and again the fingers crackled and each attack by the circling, taunting evil one left Gorwen weaker. Nor did Charn keep to any rules of fair combat.

'You're too noble, Gorwen,' he cried, picking up a large rock. 'Too noble for your own good!' And he hurled the rock, striking Gorwen on the head and causing him to stagger backwards.

The dragon recovered just in time and raised his wings to deflect the lightning that followed. But in doing so, he dropped the shoe-bag. Charn had already guessed what it must contain.

'At last,' he hissed, advancing towards it, 'the Veetons. Now *I* will be master of Pelamar . . .'

'No, never. Not whilst I live!' rumbled Gorwen, and with a mighty effort he lashed out with his tail, striking Charn and driving him back.

'But you bring me the Veetons, Gorwen,' laughed Charn. And he swirled away again, circling the weary dragon, teasing him with short, stinging flashes of green fire, until he was sure Gorwen could resist no longer. Then once more he advanced towards the precious Veetons.

'You are weak now, Gorwen . . .' he hissed, spreading his arms wide like the wings of a huge black bird of prey about to swoop for the kill. 'When I am master of Pelamar, I, Charn, Charn the evil one, will . . .'

Only there was to be no final triumph for the evil one. Because as he stood for that split second with his arms raised, he was consumed by billowing orange fire. Gorwen, summoning up his last ounce of strength, had seized his chance. And the heat of the roaring, flaming breath he directed at Charn was greater than any he had ever breathed in his life before. Even Jenny flinched from it, behind the fallen tree where she had crept to watch the battle. Charn gave a last echoing cry and disappeared in a drifting, hissing cloud of black smoke.

Gorwen stood quite still in the sudden, strange silence. Then, totally exhausted, he picked up the shoe-bag and trudged slowly towards the Veetacore House. Jenny ran to meet him.

'Gorwen . . . Gorwen . . .' She embraced the dragon tearfully and he patted her shoulder with a comforting, scaly hand.

'You've been very, very brave,' he murmured.

'So was Morris. Morris and Doris. They're both puddles, Gorwen.' Tears were getting the better of Jenny as she turned sadly to the green puddle by the fallen tree.

'Hush,' whispered the dragon. 'There may still be time . . .'

He snorted a small jet of flame gently at the puddle and, as Jenny watched, it hissed and billowed into a column of bright green vapour. And when the vapour cleared, there stood a very bewildered-looking green Keeper.

'Morris!' cried Jenny, and she hugged him tight.

Inside the Veetacore House, Gorwen performed the same life-restoring trick on the purple puddle with the glasses. Doris pretended not to like the fuss Jenny made of her, but secretly she was very flattered.

Not until the now enormous Frug had been un-puddled did the sacrifice Gorwen was making become apparent.

'Gorwen, you're fading!' cried Jenny, horrified.

'Don't do any more,' insisted Doris. 'Save your strength.'

But the dragon was already blowing on the two remaining puddles, one pink, one turquoise, on the workbench. Morris's pets, Frista and Frenny, reappeared, but Gorwen was now quite transparent.

'Now I must rest,' he whispered weakly. 'I brought two of the missing Veetons with me. Boris and the others are still looking for the last one . . .'


High on the mountainside in Widge the excitement and wonder caused by the magical waterfall of words had given way to frustration. Everyone was getting snappy as they searched in vain for the arch of brick. Then Boris's cap phone began to ring.

'Is it Jenny?' asked Amanda excitedly.

But there was no picture on the screen, only words, and they came and went, flashing brightly through the interference

before disappearing again, then finally
forming into a message:

**Charn beaten
but Gorwen fading.
Hurry!**

Scott and Amanda read the message in
silence and looked at each other helplessly.
How do you save a dying magic dragon?

The video screen in the Veetacore House
crackled and flashed violently, then went
blank.

'Well, that's that,' said Doris, shrugging
and turning away from the lifeless screen.
'Let's hope they got the message.'

Briskly she took the spherical Veeton from
the shoe-bag, while Jenny looked at the
Book and checked the diagram she had
drawn in her notebook.

'Hey, that one . . . the sphere . . .' said
Jenny, having yet another look. 'Yes,
according to the Book it should drop down

on top of the circular Veeton.'

'Well, go on. Put it in the right place then.' And Doris handed the glowing sphere to Jenny. It was the first time she had actually entrusted her with a Veeton. Jenny dropped the sphere carefully into place and smiled. The square Veeton was next. But before they could decide what to do with it, a familiar munching sound made them turn. Frug was forcing his way into a cupboard.

'Morris,' warned Doris, 'you'd better feed that caterpillar of yours . . .'


'Well, I say we should go up!'

'No! We do exactly what the waterfall said. Right?'

'Will you just shut up!' shouted Amanda. Scott and Boris stopped quarrelling in surprise.

'Okay,' said Amanda, calmly now, 'we can't find the arch. But has anyone seen any bricks at all?'

'I saw two or three,' piped up Rodey. Everyone looked at him and he added hurriedly, 'But *not* an arch.'

'*Where*?' asked Amanda.

Rodey pointed across at the sheer face of the mountain. 'Over there.'

They all went to look. There were piles of

logs all over the clearing and some were stacked vertically, propped against the mountainside where Rodey was pointing. Just above the stack of logs, several feet above head height, Scott saw what they were looking for.

'Rodey, that's it! You've found the arch!'

Rodey was bewildered. 'Three bricks? That's an arch?'

Scott knew a bit about arches. 'That big one in the middle's a keystone,' he explained, 'and all the others press on it.'

Eagerly they began to pull away the logs and throw them aside. But as Amanda grabbed a log, a strip of bark came away in her hand. There were words on the underside.

'I've found another clue!' Then her face dropped. 'No I haven't.' She showed Scott the message and he read it aloud:

> 'No more clues.
> Veetarod
> your only hope.
> Use it!'

'Well, who's got the Veetarod anyway?' asked Boris.

'I have,' said Scott, patting it. 'In my back pocket.'

Without warning, one of the remaining

logs slipped and dislodged all the others, and there in front of the search party was a complete brick arch. And beyond it, darkness.

'It's the entrance to a tunnel,' whispered Boris, peering in.

'If you must be quick, find the arch of brick,' said Amanda, remembering the waterfall of words. 'It's a short cut through the mountain!'

They all looked at each other. Boris took a torch from his rucksack. 'Well?'

'Go in, if you dare,' shrugged Amanda. 'That's what the waterfall said.'

'Right,' said Boris firmly, and he marched in, followed by Amanda.

'And it also said "Beware! Beware!"' said Scott, getting in quick behind Amanda. If he *had* to go in there, he certainly didn't want to be last.

The tunnel turned out to be all Scott feared it would be. Narrow, low, wet, winding and dark. Very dark. Beware, beware . . . But beware of what? The waterfall hadn't told them *that* . . .

'Ssh! I can hear something!' Boris had stopped. The rest of the shuffling, crouching line stopped as well. They listened anxiously, but the only sound was that of dripping water.

'Stop trying to scare us, Boris, it's stupid!' moaned Scott.

But Amanda had heard something too. And, as they listened again, they all heard it. An echoing titter, somewhere far in front of them along the tunnel. Widgets!

'They're blocking up the other end!' cried Scott. 'Well, I'm getting out of here!' And he charged blindly forward into the darkness.

A loud scream sent the others stumbling hurriedly after him, fearful of what they might find, but to their relief they found Scott still in one piece. He was standing, rigid, at the edge of a gaping hole in the tunnel floor. There was no way past it. About three metres of dark, deep nothingness lay between the search party and the end of the tunnel. Daylight winked mockingly at them through the overgrown exit, just out of reach.

'Beware of a floor that is not there . . .' whispered Boris grimly. 'The warning of Ash Rock. We'd forgotten all about that.'

'How deep is it, d'you think?' asked Amanda. She was shining the torch down into the blackness, but the beam didn't reach the bottom.

Boris dropped in a broken piece of wood. They waited a long time before they heard a faint splash far below. *Very* deep.

'Can you make your bat grow?' Amanda was hopeful, but Boris shook his head.

'No, not that long.' He considered briefly. 'But I could probably jump it. Stand back.' And, brushing aside their alarmed protests, he backpedalled down the tunnel. Amanda shut her eyes as he raced forward and took a mighty leap. When she opened them again, Boris was beaming at her from the other side of the hole.

'Wow . . .' she gasped, and Boris gave them all a little bow.

'Yes, brilliant, Boris,' grumbled Rodey, 'but *we* can't jump like that. What now?'

'Get the rope-ladder out of the rucksack

and throw one end across,' called Boris. Not only was he pleased with his long jump, he'd also done a bit of thinking ahead for once. There were wooden stumps on either side of the hole; obviously there had once been a bridge. Two stumps on each side. Ideal for securing the ends of a rope-ladder.

Rodey eyed the rope-ladder dubiously as it was tied in place. 'You're not expecting us to *walk* across this, are you?'

'No, Rodey, just swing underneath,' called Boris, as he finished the tying on his side. 'Right. Who's going first?'

'I will!' said Amanda excitedly.

Scott watched in admiration and envy as she sat on the edge of the hole and, with no more thought than if she'd been in the hall at school, took hold of the rope-ladder and swung effortlessly across, hand over hand.

'That's it. Well done,' said Boris. 'Right, Rodey, you're next—and bring the rucksack.'

While Rodey struggled across, Amanda walked quickly on to the tunnel exit and peered out. But there was nothing to see. Nothing but dense mist. She could hear the voices of Boris and Rodey behind her.

'Come on, Rodey. Swing!'

'Swing . . . I'm a mouse not a monkey!'

But Rodey made it in the end, and that left only Scott.

The first few rungs weren't too bad. But then Scott lost his rhythm and no matter how hard he tried he couldn't get it back. He was stuck, dangling in space.

'My arms hurt! I'm going to fall!'

Scott wriggled desperately like a fish on a hook while Boris tried to haul him in. At last an orange fist closed over Scott's arm.

'Come on, that's it . . . come on. Swing your feet up . . . Walk up the wall . . .'

Scott managed to do as he was told. But as his feet reached firm, level ground, he felt something slip from his back pocket.

'The Veetarod!' he shrieked. And for a moment everyone froze. Then the silence was broken by a splash, far, far below.

# Danger on high!

It was the worst moment of Scott's life. And Rodey didn't make it any better.

'You heard what the last message said!' cried the mouse. 'Read it again, Amanda.'

Reluctantly, Amanda unfurled the bark message. 'No more clues. Veetarod your only hope. Use it.'

'Yes!' Rodey stamped his foot. 'Our *only* hope. Sunk!'

'How d'you know it's sunk?' retorted Amanda, sticking up for Scott. 'It could've floated.'

Rodey wasn't impressed. 'So what if it did float? How do you propose to get it up again—go fishing?'

'Yes.' Amanda turned to Boris. 'We'll need the rest of your jumper.'

'Why?' Boris looked at her, puzzled, then realised what she was getting at. It was a great shame to unravel the remains of such a magnificent garment, but when you are on a quest, sacrifices have to be made . . .

'Scott, look in the rucksack,' said Amanda. 'See if there's anything we can tie it to. Let's try and scoop up the Veetarod.'

'That won't work,' scoffed Rodey. 'We

could be swishing about for hours.'

Scott had found a small two-handled pan in the rucksack. Rodey took it from him and thrust it at Boris. 'Tie the thread onto that,' he said, 'I'm going down in it.'

Amanda realised what was in the mouse's mind. 'You mustn't shrink, Rodey!' she cried. 'You might never grow big again.'

But Rodey was already thinking small, his paws over his eyes.

'I should've been a frog, not a mouse,' he muttered, then he shimmered and shrank.

Amanda stooped and gently lifted the tiny white mouse into the pan.

'Thank you. Lower away, Boris.'

Boris had tied one end of the jumper thread to the handles of the pan and now, with Rodey on board, he began to lower the pan carefully over the edge of the hole.

Rodey sat very still. Whenever he moved, the pan seemed to tilt and sway dangerously. Being lowered down was bad enough, but being tipped out and falling . . . His whiskers trembled at the thought. He couldn't see the others clearly now. They were just small, dark shapes high above him. Getting smaller and darker all the time.

'Are you at the bottom yet, Rodey?' Boris's voice was a small echo.

'No, not yet.'

'I've got plenty more string left.'

'Thank you,' said Rodey, hoping that plenty more string wouldn't be necessary. But it was . . .

He felt the water at the bottom before he saw it. The string suddenly went slack and the pan slapped and jolted, tossing him sideways.

'Stop!' he squeaked, as loose string began to coil around him.

'Can you see it?' called Boris excitedly.

Rodey steadied himself, waited for the pan to stop bobbing about, then peered over the side. He could see very little in the

faint light. Then he saw the Veetarod, floating nearby like a golden raft.

'Yes—there it is!'

'Can you *reach* it?' called Boris.

'I'll try . . .'

It was a risky business. Though folded, the Veetarod was still far bigger than Rodey himself. And when he reached out for it, the pan tilted wildly, almost toppling him head first into the water. By shifting his weight he managed to float the pan closer to the Veetarod, getting right alongside before trying again.

High above, the others could see nothing of Rodey's efforts deep down in the darkness, only hear his occasional squeaks of alarm. And then, at last, a tiny, breathless call:

'Got it . . .'

Rodey lay exhausted in the bottom of the pan, the dripping Veetarod propped precariously beside him, its weight causing the pan to list dangerously. Boris's anxious voice echoed down to him.

'Are you all right?'

'Yes . . .' gasped the mouse. 'Haul me up, quick.'

Gradually the small dark shapes became faces again. Anxious faces at first, then beaming, relieved, delighted faces, as the pan came swaying up into the dim light of the tunnel.

'Rodey, you're a hero!' cried Amanda, scooping him up.

'A super-hero!' grinned Scott, more grateful than he could say, and he turned to Boris and handed him the Veetarod rather shamefacedly. 'Here, Boris. You'd better put this in the rucksack.'

'No,' said Boris firmly. 'We're going to need it. *You* keep it.' Then he grinned. 'But not in your back pocket!'


'When it's working, does this bit spin round?' asked Jenny. She was studying the inside of the Veetacore.

'I don't know,' pondered Doris. 'I've never seen the inside before. Try it.'

Jenny touched the glowing centre of the Veetacore and it spun gently, smooth and perfectly balanced. She and Doris gazed at it, fascinated.

Morris was glad they were so engrossed. He had heard that ominous munching sound again and turned to find Frug on the Book stand.

'Frug, get off!' he whispered urgently, and heaved him away before Doris and Jenny noticed.

134

'Now let's see what else we've got,' said Doris briskly. 'Eight more Veetons. Morris, where's the Book?'

'I don't think we need the Book any more,' said Morris guiltily. At least, it was guilt about Frug that made him say it, but the more he thought about it, the more obvious it seemed to be.

'Just think of the Veetacore's shape,' he went on, hugging the giant caterpillar as he spoke. 'One side's the same as the other. Like Frug will be.'

'What *are* you babbling about?' sighed Doris.

'Have you ever seen a butterfly with different shaped wings? Butterflies are the same on both sides, aren't they?' said Morris.

It was Jenny who began to cotton on first.

'So the Veetacore . . .'

'. . . is the same on both sides,' cried Morris. He had put Frug down on the floor now and was over by the Veetacore, pretending to carve a line through its centre. 'Just like a butterfly's body: everything on this side should be exactly the same as on that side.'

'Why didn't you say so in the first place,' said Doris.

But then the munching started again.

'What are you eating *now*, Frug!' cried Morris, hurrying across to haul him out of a cupboard. It turned out to be one of Boris's best tennis shoes.

'Oh *when* will you start spinning your cocoon?' Morris asked despairingly. 'Don't you *want* to be a beautiful butterfly?'

Gorwen stirred slightly and they all turned anxiously towards him.

'It's all right, Gorwen,' said Jenny softly, 'we've nearly done it.'

But the fading dragon made no further sound or movement.


'Widge mist. The worst kind,' said Boris, as the search party stood at the tunnel exit, peering uneasily into the wispy grey gloom. Scott was holding the Veetarod and there was no doubt which way *that* wanted to go. Scott turned to Amanda.

'That's what the Ash Rock message said: Beware of a floor that isn't there, then climb on *up* again.'

So uphill they went. Into the dense mist. Amanda with the exhausted Rodey in her pocket, Boris with the bat and rucksack, Scott with the Veetarod. They clasped each other's hands for safety, like mountaineers roping themselves together. And all around them squeals of laughter drifted eerily out of the mist.

'Take no notice of the Widgets,' said Boris firmly, as they edged carefully forward. 'As long as we can feel the ground sloping up, we're going the right way.'

'I can hear something else,' said Amanda.

Boris listened. 'Sounds like running water. It must be a spring.'

And a spring it was, bubbling out of the ground just above them. After a few more paces the ground levelled out, the mist swirled away, and bright warm sunshine lit up their faces. They had reached the top of the mountain.

Amanda and Scott just stood for a moment, half admiring the view, half expecting to find the last Veeton sitting on a rock waiting for them. Boris was surprised to find he was still holding a hand. And still more surprised to find that the hand was small and furry. His Widget companion twirled and tittered, then skipped away downhill into the mist. Boris hitched up the heavy rucksack on his shoulders and joined Scott and Amanda by the spring.

It had been a stiff climb and they were all tired and thirsty. A short rest was in order, no matter how excited the Veetarod was getting. But as Boris picked up his rucksack again, he saw a group of Widgets playing tug of war with something a little way off at the edge of the mountain. Boris froze and his voice came out as a dry whisper.

'Oh no . . . not my bat . . . Not my bat . . . Please not my bat!'

He made to charge off, but Amanda grabbed his arm.

'Wait, Boris! They might drop it over the edge.'

'Those Widgets!' roared Boris, shaking her off.

'Boris! If they lose it, we can't get home again!'

Boris calmed down slightly. 'Well there's

no point just *asking* them,' he said, glaring balefully across at the capering, squeaking band of troublemakers. 'They won't just *give* it back.'

'Let's swap it for something,' suggested Scott.

'For what?'

'Some of your new books?' Amanda was looking at Boris.

'My *books*?' Boris thought again of that magical moment in the Book Tree when the Tree itself had given them to him. They had looked so interesting. So exciting. Far too good for Widgets.

'Let's write them a note,' said Scott. 'We know they can read.'

The Widgets' tug of war had now become a general scrummage as they pushed, shoved and tickled each other in their attempts to gain personal possession of the bat. They all looked up as Scott approached and showed them the message in the notebook:

Let's swap

The books for the bat.

But when Boris held out some books, the Widgets all shook their heads.

'More?' asked Amanda, giving Boris more

books from the rucksack. Scott wrote 'More?' in his notebook, but still the Widgets weren't satisfied. Amanda delved in the rucksack yet again. This time when Boris sadly held out the offering, the Widgets nodded and rushed forward. Boris immediately clutched the books to his chest.

'No bat, no books,' said Amanda sternly, and she held out her hand.

Both sides stared at each other warily as the Widget with the bat slowly held it up. Then, when Amanda's hand closed on it, Boris held out the books again and they were grabbed excitedly by the Widgets, who turned and scampered off. Boris watched them wistfully as they all settled down on the mountain top, each with their very own book.

Amanda smiled and handed the bat to the orange Keeper. 'Cheer up, Boris. There's still a bundle left.'


'There,' said Morris, standing back proudly, 'it's really looking like the Veetacore now.'

He had been right about it being the same on both sides, and now only two pieces remained to be fitted. But one of those was still somewhere in Widge . . .

At least they didn't have to worry about

140

Frug eating the Book any more. He was hanging on the wall.

'How long will he stay in this cocoon, now he's finally made it?' asked Jenny.

'Oh,' said Morris vaguely, 'you never can tell.'

Doris banged down Gorwen's videophone. She had been crouching beside the almost invisible dragon, trying in vain to contact Boris. She was angry and upset. 'Oh, Gorwen . . .' And to Jenny's amazement, the proud purple Keeper burst into tears.

'Don't cry, Doris. Here, let me have a go.' Jenny hurried over to her.

'It's just not working any more,' said Doris. '*Nothing's* working.'

'One more try,' Jenny insisted, and she started to press buttons. 'Come on, Boris, answer, *please* . . .'


The mountain top in Widge was not so much a peak as a ridge. Or, to be precise, two ridges, with a deep, steep-sided ravine between them. Scott, Amanda and Boris were following the Veetarod along their ridge, away from the spring, when Boris became aware of a faint buzzing in his head. So feeble and unfamiliar was the sound that it took him several seconds to realise what was making it. His cap phone. He pulled his cap off and gazed at the flickering screen.

'Is that you, Jenny?'

'Boris . . . can you hear me?' The voice was as faint and fuzzy as the image on the screen. 'Did you get our message about Gorwen? He's almost gone. You must find the last Veeton or it'll be too late to save him . . .' The screen was already blank before the voice gave up as well.

'Boris! There it is!'

Scott's shout made Boris look up. Amanda was pointing with the Veetarod towards a strange, creeper-like tree, growing out over the ravine. Precariously wedged in the furthermost branch was a cylindrical Veeton.

'But we can't get *that*,' whispered Scott, as the three of them stood and stared.

'We've *got* to,' said Boris. 'Quickly. Gorwen's almost gone!'

Scott hesitated, then leapt forward and started to climb the tree. Crawling out along its twisted trunk. Into space. He kept his eyes fixed on the Veeton, trying not to dislodge it by moving too clumsily, trying not to dislodge himself either. Inch by inch he got closer, never looking down, never thinking about anything except the next hand-hold. At last he judged he was close enough and reached out. But as his fingers closed around the Veeton, there was a sharp crack and the noise of splitting wood, and the branch he was clinging to lurched downwards.

'Scott!' screamed Amanda.

# 10 The final page

There was nothing Amanda or Boris could do. Scott was stuck, hanging headfirst in space, the last Veeton slipping from his fingers, and they were helpless. If they tried to climb out along the tree after him, their extra weight would certainly cause the branch to break altogether. Scott and the Veeton would be gone. Forever.

Rescue came from an unexpected source. A group of Widgets, picnicking on the far side of the ravine, sat up when they heard Amanda's terrified scream. Instantly they were on their furry feet, gathering up their tablecloth and signalling to their book-reading friends on the other side to hurry to the tree. One end of the tablecloth was then thrown across and, as the branch cracked again, both sets of Widgets moved sideways so that the cloth hung beneath the tree.

Scott didn't understand Widgeon, but it was pretty clear that the urgent chippering coming from both sides meant 'Let go!' But was this just another Widget trick? Were they going to whip the cloth away just as he fell into it? He felt the branch splitting still further. Trick or not, he was going to fall anyway. He shut his eyes, clutched the Veeton and let go of the tree.

He felt the cloth give way beneath him as he landed on it. Suddenly it snapped taut and catapulted him high into the air like some magical trampoline. He glimpsed the astonished Amanda and Boris far below as he somersaulted, then fell like a stone. The narrow white cloth seemed to rush up to meet him, but the Widgets stood firm, holding it tight as he landed and bounced again, even higher this time, before twisting in mid-air and somehow landing on his feet—right beside Amanda.

'We got it,' said Scott, in a daze, 'the last Veeton . . .' And he was immediately mobbed by celebrating Widgets.

'*You* got it,' grinned Boris. 'You and the Widgets .' He took the nearest paw and shook it. 'Thank you.'

'Yes, thank you,' said Amanda, shaking another. And suddenly the mountain top was alive with shake-paw, a brand new Widget game, which involved shaking everyone else's hand as often and rapidly as possible, preferably while squealing, laughing and falling over.

'Look, Boris!' cried Amanda, as the search party eventually managed to ease their way out of the furry scrum.

Boris looked where she was pointing. The
Widgets on the other side of the ravine were
holding up their tablecloth like a banner.
On it they had written 'Goodbye! Good
Luck!' But Amanda was staring wide-eyed at
the thinks bubbles which had popped up as
well:

*Goodbye!*

*See you!*

'Oh, they do that all the time,' shrugged
Boris.

The bubbles popped as Scott and Amanda
waved farewell.

'Told you the Widgets were all right,' said
Boris, picking up his rucksack.

'Power of good
spread near and far.
Power of good
give life to Pelamar . . .'

Jenny looked up sadly from the spell in the
Book. Life to Pelamar . . . Would there be
life left in Gorwen? Parts of him had
disappeared altogether now. Even Doris and
Morris were becoming deathly pale.

The twenty-fourth Veeton was in place.

146

There was nothing left to do but wait. Wait and watch the cracks that had begun to appear in the Veetacore House . . .


'Remember the last time we were here?' grinned Amanda.

The search party had stopped to rest on their long trek back through Widge. It was dark now, but the clearing they had stopped in was still familiar.

'Yes,' said Boris, looking towards it fondly. 'That's my Book Tree . . .' He turned to Amanda, remembering something else. 'How's Rodey?'

The mouse was still fast asleep in Amanda's pocket. Scott wished *he* was asleep. He felt tired and ratty. His legs ached, his feet were sore and in his heart of hearts he feared all this hurrying was for nothing anyway. They were going to be too late. Amanda was beginning to droop as well.

'Come on,' said Boris, very brightly, 'let's sing something. It'll cheer us up.'

But nobody wanted to.

'Come on . . . Who's going to start?'

Boris had barely asked the question when the door of the Book Tree flew open and yellow light streamed across the clearing.

'The trees will start,' said the Tree. 'The trees of Widge will sing you home . . .'

The three adventurers stared and listened. And although they could hear no words, nor really see the leaves or branches of the forest move, they became aware of *something*. Something in their hearts. Hope. Renewed strength. A fresh sense of urgency. So that shortly afterwards, Scott and Amanda found themselves striding eagerly along the path again, without even remembering having stood up.

Through the night they marched without further rest. There was no moon, no stars, the torch in Amanda's hand became dim; but not once did they stumble or lose their way. Only when their trek was almost complete did the 'song' in their hearts fade away and doubt and tiredness take its place again.

'*I* don't think we're on the right path,' muttered Scott. 'We crossed the Bog of Boris ages ago . . .'

'There!' cried Amanda. 'That's the rock Boris sat on when we arrived in Widge! And that's the Widgets' camp-fire!' She was running forward excitedly. 'We're almost back in Pelamar. We can fly!'

But could they? Boris's bat would need to carry three passengers, not just the two it had brought to Widge. And even Boris was growing paler now. Would his magic work?

'Length, bat, length.' He clicked his fingers, but nothing happened. 'Length, bat, length!' he repeated, tensely.

For a moment it seemed there would still be no response, then the bat shimmered and grew. Boris blew a sigh of relief and put the torch and the Veeton in his rucksack. Then he arranged Scott and Amanda at either end of the bat before taking up position himself in the middle.

'Right,' he said, 'pick up the bat . . . Now, when I say run, you run. Ready ? Run!'

And holding the bat in front of them, they raced across the clearing. It seemed to Scott they must hit the trees on the far side, but at the last moment the bat whisked them into the air, their toes brushing the topmost branches as they flashed by. Boris leaned slightly to the right and the bat banked steeply, pulling them round in a broad arc before heading across the moonlit sky towards Pelamar.

Morris, Doris and Jenny were standing anxiously by a large crack in the wall of the Veetacore House.

'It *is* wider, isn't it?' said Doris, as Jenny measured.

Jenny looked at her notebook. At 7.30 pm she had written 'one thumb nail'. Now the crack was twice that wide.

'Yes, a bit,' she answered, trying to sound less worried than she actually was.

'Come on, bat . . . You're slowing down.' Boris knew he had asked a lot of the trusty bat. But then, the quest had asked a lot of everyone—and everything. He was desperately tired himself and he could see that Scott and Amanda were too. They

150

needed the 'song of the trees' again, to keep them going. But there was little chance of that high in the night sky . . .

'Look, Boris!' cried Scott. 'Star signs . . .'

All around them, shooting, bursting stars whizzed and glowed, and each of the three travellers clinging to the bat saw the word that formed ahead of them and shone brightest of all: Pelamar. They smiled at each other and gripped the bat even tighter.


> 7.30 pm—one thumb nail
> 9.30 pm—one thumb joint
> 11.30 pm—

Jenny turned quietly before measuring the crack in the wall again. Doris was asleep at the table, slumped over the Book. Morris was dozing in his rocking chair. That was good. Jenny measured the crack and her fears were confirmed. *Two* thumb joints wide . . .

'Oh, Gorwen,' she whispered, 'they can't be much longer now . . .'


The sun was rising over Pelamar, but the change from night to day made no difference to the landscape except to change dark grey to light grey. There was no green left at all now. And no other colour either.

'Doesn't it look awful,' said Amanda sadly. 'Are we too late?'

Boris didn't answer immediately. He was straining his eyes towards the horizon. At last he saw what he was hoping to see.

'Look, the Veetacore House is still there.'

But as he spoke, the bat suddenly dropped sideways, its flying power completely spent, and the cries of its passengers spiralled down with it as it fell to earth.

'Right, that's it,' sighed Boris grimly, struggling to his feet. 'No more flying.'

Amanda scrambled to the top of the bank where they had landed. 'The Veetacore House!' she cried, pointing. 'It's over there. Miles away. Boris, what can we do?'

Boris looked down at the bat lying on the ground. 'It's up to you, old friend,' he said quietly.

Scott frowned. 'I thought you said it couldn't fly any more?'

'It can't,' said Boris. Then without further explanation, he clicked his fingers. 'Wheels, bat, wheels.' And before them stood a long, bat-shaped skateboard with three sets of wheels. It looked fast and ready for action.

Drained of colour, like the meadow outside, Doris slowly closed the window shutters and turned towards Jenny and Morris, who were sitting listlessly at the table.

'It's no good,' said Doris in a flat, quiet voice, 'they're not coming. Pelamar's finished.' She looked across at Gorwen, or what remained of him, which seemed little more than a wisp of grey transparent gauze. 'We nearly did it, didn't we, Gorwen . . .'

Then the doors crashed open behind her and a giant skateboard burst into the Veetacore House, its three riders leaping off and dashing towards her.

'Boris!' cried Doris, too astonished to feel relief, joy or anything else.

'Quick . . . take it!' yelled Boris, wriggling the rucksack from his back.

Jenny rushed to help, but Doris had quickly recovered from her astonishment and was already tugging the Veeton out of the rucksack. 'The Book, Jenny!' she cried. 'Which way up does this one go?'

Jenny quickly opened the Book and turned to the last page. Only to get a shock even greater than her very first sight of Charn.

'The last page! It's gone—Frug's eaten it!'

Everyone stood quite still, just staring at her.

Morris spoke first. 'He can't have . . . Not *all* of it . . .'

Jenny read aloud. 'Warning! The marked end of the central cylinder must . . .' Then she looked up and shrugged helplessly. 'That's all. The rest's gone.'

'Oh, Frug!' Morris was standing by the cocoon now. His voice was an agonised whisper. But as he ran his finger sadly down its hard, rough casing, the cocoon split from top to bottom, revealing a giant furled butterfly, its body pale green, its wings transparent and glistening.

Gradually the butterfly began to free itself

from the cocoon and its wings opened to their full span.

'Look at its wings,' whispered Boris. 'They've got words on them . . .'

Amanda had seen as well. 'Yeah . . . Words from the Book?'

Then, as if a spell cast by the huge, beautiful butterfly had been broken, they all rushed forward.

'Don't touch him!' Morris cried anxiously. 'He's very fragile.'

The butterfly had fluttered to the top of the Veetacore.

'Other!' read Amanda. 'One of the words is "other". Quick, write it down, Jenny!'

'And "touch"!' called Scott.

Now the butterfly was on the Book stand. Squinting sideways, Doris recognised a third word.

'Veetons!'

The butterfly moved again, clearly anxious to be outside. Boris pushed the window shutters fully open for it and read the last word as the butterfly flew past him and away.

'Never. Yes, "never"!'

'This is the marked end,' said Doris, examining the Veeton and finding a cross.

Jenny was scanning the words she had written in her notebook with increasing

desperation. 'Other, touch, Veetons, never
. . . Touch Veetons never? . . . Never touch
Veetons!' Yes, that was it! 'Other Veetons!'

'The marked end must never touch other
Veetons!' cried Doris, turning the Veeton
marked end up. 'Boris! Morris!'

Solemnly the three Keepers marched to
the Veetacore and carefully lowered the
twenty-fifth Veeton into place, chanting the
spell as they did so:

> 'Power of good
> spread near and far.
> Power of good
> give life to Pelamar.
>
> Banish evil thoughts,
> banish evil ways.
> Make a world full of good
> from the Veetacore's rays.'

For a moment nothing happened, then
the Veetacore began to glow, and with the
glow began a humming sound. A deep,
powerful hum, full of strength and the
power of life. And the golden light of the
Veetacore became so bright that it dazzled
the children and they had to move away.

'We've done it!' shouted Boris, his arms
raised in triumph, his face and hands
flushed orange again.

'Look outside!' Amanda turned to the window. The meadow beyond was no longer grey but green. Green and brown. Green and brown and pink and yellow . . . A flood of colour seemed to be washing across the landscape as far as the eye could see.

But what about Gorwen? Children and Pelamots paused in their joyful, tearful embracing and looked to where the shadow that had once been a noble dragon rested.

'Gorwen's coming back!' Jenny was certain she wasn't imagining it.

As they watched, and wished, the missing parts of the dragon began to reappear.

'Come on, you can make it,' urged Boris.

'Of course he'll make it,' Doris said proudly. 'He's a Pelamot.'

Gorwen was becoming solid now, his colour changing from grey to dragon green. 'Yes,' he rumbled, 'I am a Pelamot!' And a breath of smoke curled from his nostrils.

'Gorwen!' Amanda and Jenny both threw their arms around his scaly neck.

Doris was quite overcome. 'Morris!' she sniffed. 'Where's the Pelamade? The *special* Pelamade.'

Then Amanda's jacket pocket began to bulge and wriggle. She had forgotten Rodey again. But she hardly had time to put her hand in her pocket to pull him out before there he was, shimmering and growing to full Pelamot size beside her.

'Join the party!' cried Boris.

And a fine party it was. Morris had produced two large cobweb-covered bottles from a cupboard.

'This is the *special* Pelamade,' he announced proudly. 'We've been saving it for a special day. But we never thought it would be as special as this!'

When everyone's glass had been filled with the rich, red liquid, Doris cleared her throat and spoke. 'The Keepers, and all your friends in Pelamar, say thank you. Thank you, Scott, Jenny and Amanda.'

'Scott, Jenny and Amanda!' As one, the
Pelamots raised their glasses and drank the
toast. All was well again in the land of
Pelamar. But as everyone laughed and
chattered, Amanda became aware of a
sound that had nothing to do with Pelamar.
Distant at first, but then close by.

'That was the dinner whistle!' she said.

'It can't have been,' frowned Scott.

But Jenny had heard it too. 'It was. One
for break, two for dinner.'

'Yeah,' said Scott, almost in dismay, 'but
not *here*, not in Pelamar . . .'

As he spoke, the walls of the Veetacore
House seemed to melt around him and in

their place stood school and the playground wall. The mural was still there, so were the brushes and pots of paint. And Miss Taylor.

'Well done,' she smiled, standing behind them, admiring their handiwork. The dragon in the mural winked. Miss Taylor saw it. But was quite sure she could *not* have seen it. Painted dragons don't wink. She glanced at the children, turned away and blew her whistle again.

'Pack up now,' she said, and left them gazing at the dragon. *Their* dragon. It winked again and Scott felt hurriedly in his pocket. His notebook was still there—and something else. A tiny cylinder of gold. Jenny and Amanda each had one as well: Jenny a sphere, Amanda a square. Their own miniature Veetons, glowing in their hands.

'It *was* real,' whispered Scott. 'Thank you, Gorwen . . .'

They all looked up at the mural. A banner was fluttering above the white house with the green doors. There were words on it:

# *The End*

Yes, it *had* all really happened. In the wink of a dragon's eye . . .